The Billionaire's Christmas Vows

A Jet City Billionaire Christmas Romance

Gina Robinson

Gina Robinson
SEATTLE, WASHINGTON

Also by
GINA ROBINSON

SWITCHED AT MARRIAGE ROMANCE
SERIAL
Part 1, A WEDDING TO REMEMBER
Part 2, THE VIRGIN BILLIONAIRE
Part 3, TO HAVE AND TO HOLD
Part 4, FROM THIS DAY FORWARD
Part 5, FOR RICHER, FOR RICHEST
Part 6, IN SICKNESS AND IN WEALTH
Part 7, TO LOVE AND TO CHERISH

NEW ADULT ROMANCE
RUSHED
CRUSHED
HUSHED
RECKLESS LONGING
RECKLESS SECRETS
RECKLESS TOGETHER

THE AGENT EX SERIES
"Full of laughter, intrigue, and, of course, steamy
spies." —*RT Book Reviews*

LICENSE TO LOVE
THE SPY WHO LEFT ME
DIAMONDS ARE TRULY FOREVER
LIVE AND LET LOVE
LOVE ANOTHER DAY

CHAPTER ONE

Cyber Monday, December 1st

Kayla

Like most self-made billionaires, my husband was a workaholic. That stereotype about billionaires jetting around the world on vacation or cruising idly on their yachts for months at a time? Myth. If you wanted to stay a billionaire, anyway. No one I knew wanted to lose that third hard-won comma in their net worth.

The only yachting we were going to be doing this holiday season was on Lake Washington past our lakefront home. As part of the Christmas Ships Parade Friday night. On our friend, and Justin's business partner, Riggins Feldhem's yacht. At his invitation. His yacht. His party. A Seattle tradition.

I was looking forward to participating from the water on a private yacht this year, rather than as a landlocked bystander onshore in a crowded public park. I would be drinking a hand-mixed cocktail instead of clutching my usual Styrofoam cup of watered-down Swiss Miss. The perks of being married to a billionaire and hanging with his young, hot billionaire buds.

I just hoped I didn't have to go solo to the party because Jus was working. Jus was cofounder of one of Seattle's fastest growing online retail operations, Flashionista. And this was their busy season.

Since agreeing to play the part of Justin Green's wife six months ago, I'd gotten to know more than a few billionaires. Like so many other successful execs, even when they were vacationing, they were working.

Multibillion-dollar companies didn't run themselves. And your competitors were always out to get you one way or another. Out-innovate. Outsell. Outsmart. Outmaneuver. And in retail, undercut.

On no other day was that more true than the most vicious online retail day of the year, Cyber Monday. While savvy customers rushed to snap up the best deals of the year, a retail war for their dollars raged. This year, Thanksgiving had been one day short of the latest it could possibly be. Which had Jus, and everyone in retail, "concerned," as he liked to put it. Which, translated from guy-speak, meant panicked. Fewer than normal high-volume sales days to get out of the red and into the black.

With the short season, the competition was going to be fiercer than *ever*. *Bring out the pots of boiling oil,* men! Make sure our prices are rock bottom, our ads the catchiest, and our loss leaders the hottest deals on the planet! We must fight back the retail attackers!*

Jus wasn't the only one stressing. I was panicked about the unusually brief holiday season, too. So much to do! So many presents to buy and parties to plan. So *little* time.

In my first holiday season as a billionaire's wife, and pregnant, I felt the usual holiday stress, magnified a mere *one hundred times or so.*

I was expected to plan and/or host so many parties, my head spun—one for the Flash execs and upper management; one for our friends and family; one for the children at the children's hospital; one for the employees at Flash. The last one I was simply helping Justin's new assistant with. He'd fired his last assistant in September. She was now awaiting trial for a variety of crimes related to her obsession with Jus.

And given the lift in my financial status, I was also certain my friends and family were expecting particularly expensive, and thoughtful, gifts this year. I prided myself on taking the time to find the perfect present for each person on my list. I had a reputation, and expectations, to maintain. Like Santa, I didn't want to let anyone down. No one on my list rated a lump of coal or anything remotely close.

I could handle most of it. Probably. Except for Jus. What did I get the man I loved beyond measure? Who meant more to me than anyone else? What do you give a billionaire? An "our first Christmas together" ornament, even dipped in gold, wasn't going to cut it.

I sat at my kitchen table, facing Lake Washington, with a steaming, freshly made peppermint mocha and my phone in front of me, repeatedly refreshing and checking the deals on the Flashionista website. Just, you know, to make sure all of Justin's hard work ensuring the site could handle that extra holiday traffic had paid off. And that Flashionista.com was running smoothly. Never mind that I was probably doing my share of weighing it down with all my refreshing and browsing.

So many cute things! So many fabulous deals. A silver tassel necklace that would look *fantastic* with the new blouse I'd just bought. A shiny maroon satchel handbag with a kiss-lock closure. Who didn't love a kiss-lock closure? Even the sound of it was romantic.

Shiny things. Shiny things *everywhere* just in time for Christmas. I *wanted.*

And look at the adorable baby clothes. My finger trembled as it hovered over the "add to cart/buy now" button.

If I hadn't been Justin's wife, I would have been scooping them up and maxing out my high-limit black credit card. Of course, I wouldn't have had the high-limit card to begin with. Details! As it was, I was under strict instructions from Jus *to leave the deals for the customers, babe.*

Scrooge.

I made a mental note to ask the merchandise buyers if any samples of these adorable handbags were going to find their way into the fabulous, fantastic, stupendous annual employee-only Santa Sample Sale I was managing on December 23rd. Couldn't I just buy one? So many women on my list would love it!

Magda, my excellent housekeeper and cook, made the best peppermint mocha around. But I drank it distractedly, barely tasting it. Jus had been upgrading Flashionista.com since September, and preparing it for the increased holiday traffic they were hoping for. I crossed my fingers the site didn't crash. Cyber Monday sales would keep the company in the black for a full year and allow Jus to grow the company the way he envisioned.

Jus and Riggins founded Flashionista several years ago while Jus was still in his teens. It had gone public earlier in the year. After the IPO, they maintained the majority share.

Flash, as we called it, was a strictly online retail site that catered to the under-forty, mostly female crowd who loved bargains, boutique fashions that made them stand out as stylish and unique, and had practically no time in their hectic lives to shop except online. Busy career women. Young moms. College women on limited budgets. The limited-quantity deals on Flash lasted only a few days and sold out quickly, often before noon.

Since September, Flash had been in peak season. It was getting so I hated that word "peak" with a passion bordering on obsession. Everything could be blamed on it. Everything *was* blamed on it. And every understanding was expected *because* of it. It had made me a work widow.

Vacation and personal time-off days were on blackout until the retail dead zone of mid-January. Overtime was not only authorized, but expected and practically mandated. And our first Thanksgiving as a married couple had been a disaster because of it. In my opinion, at least.

A quick slice of turkey, three olives, a bite of yams, and half a roll at his parents' house, all before two in the afternoon.

No time to linger! No time for *more*. Hurry, hurry, hurry! Must dash to my parents' house across town like skittering reindeer.

Gobble, gobble a mouthful of my mom's famous whipped pumpkin pie topped with honey whipped cream. Down a quick holiday toast.

Jus, feeling guilty for not being in the office for the *entire* day—damn those Thanksgiving Day bargains—was out the door for the Flash offices before halftime of the second football game of the day. Leaving me to feel decidedly single and lonely again.

At least he left me at my parents' house, not his. Though his family loved me, as a newlywed, I still preferred the comfort and familiarity of mine. And our own holiday routine.

I hadn't seen Jus since. He'd been working 24/7, catching naps here and there and sleeping at the office. At least that's what he told me. I had no reason to doubt him. But in my pregnancy hormoned-up state, it was easy to feel all kinds of slights, even imaginary ones. And even a little jealous. Hey, if he could blame everything on peak, I could blame my hormones without guilt.

The baby kicked. I rubbed my nearly six-month baby bump and cooed to calm the baby. If Justin's absence kept up, this baby would be born not knowing the sound of her daddy's voice. At least she wouldn't be born during peak. Can you imagine the horror of that?

In my family, Thanksgiving kicked off the holiday season with a well-established succession of events. Mom decorated and cooked as if she were Martha Stewart. Her house looked like it should have been in a holiday edition of a women's magazine. And we never ate Thanksgiving dinner before seven. Eating pie at three in the afternoon? Unheard of! And a testimony to how much my parents loved Jus that they were willing to bend on that and eat pie before dinner.

On a typical Thanksgiving, after dinner, if my physician father wasn't called out on an emergency, we watched our first Christmas movie of the season. One of our old favorites. Or a new one, if one was out.

On Black Friday, Mom and I rose in the middle of the night and hit the sales. All those stores opening on Thanksgiving evening had eroded the thrills and crowds of the Black Fridays I remembered as a girl, not to mention taken my husband away from me even earlier on Thanksgiving Day. But Black Friday was still fun and steeped with tradition for us—shopping, breakfast out, home to put up the tree.

This year, however, I had been under strict orders by Jus not to put up the tree. It was too dangerous for a pregnant woman whose balance was off. He'd hired a designer who came in on Friday and Saturday, and decorated not only *the* tree, but three trees and the rest of the house.

Jus came into the marriage with several houses and a penthouse. Until October, we'd been living in the penthouse in Bellevue. But because we were expecting a family, Jus and I relocated to his Italianate mansion on Lake Washington. Which explained the three trees. We probably could have done even a couple more, but I drew the line at three. Oh, and did I mention the expert outdoor lighting expert and landscaper who put up our outdoor lights and decorated our grounds for Christmas?

Everything looked lovely. Jus had left all the decorating decisions to me. And while on one level it was exciting, and a dream come true, getting the perfect look, doing it without Jus made the season feel hollow. Was this the way the holidays would always be? Jus missing in action during the happiest time of year?

I missed Jus more than I ever imagined I could. Something about him just made everyone smile. Me, most of all. Jus was that sweet kind of guy that took a girl's breath away when he grinned. Or walked into a room. Or breathed.

I put the finishing touch, my own little Christmas drawing of mistletoe and holly, on the box in front of me. It was packed and ready for the pickup to be delivered to Jus at his office later in the day. I'd wanted to make his holidays special and remind him how much I loved him while he was so crazy busy he could barely think. I'd racked my brain for the perfect thing. And come up with one of those advent calendars for grownups from Seattle's major coffee company.

This year's was a magnetic chalkboard covered with tins, each with a date on it for December 1st-24th. Inside each tin was a little treat—a coupon for a cup of coffee, a chocolate-covered espresso bean, a small cookie for dunking. Jus drank coffee and energy drinks to keep him running the long hours. Flash had their own coffee shop on the ground floor of the offices. So the coffee advent calendar was perfect for him.

I'd added my own touches. Little love notes. Download codes for the Christmas song of the day. That kind of thing.

I shouldn't have been insecure. Jus had had a crush on me long before I fell in love with him. The thing was, even though I was Justin's "wife", I'd never married him. He'd hired me to play his spouse for a year after being drugged in Reno and "marrying" a woman who'd forged *my* signature on the marriage license. Married without a prenup, I might add. Bad, bad news for a billionaire.

Jus didn't remember any of it. While Jus and I were pretending to be in love to sell the fake marriage as genuine, I fell in love with him. We fell in love with each other. And decided to stay "married."

In another strange twist, I'd known Jus in college when he was a young, geeky, techie genius who should have still been in high school. Four years later, when he proposed an arrangement where I pretended to be his wife for a year, he'd become the proverbial ugly duckling who was now filthy rich. All he'd needed was a little encouragement from me in the fashion and style department, and he'd turned completely into a hot swan.

Jus was colorblind and didn't care much about fashion, which was especially ironic given the company he'd founded. But he had the body and the bone structure to pull off any look. It just needed to be showcased properly.

So now here we were, pretending to be married for the rest of our lives. We had never exchanged vows. But, due to that clever forgery and my assertion that it was my signature, our marriage was legal as far as the state was concerned.

Before I "married" Jus, I'd dreamed of a big, beautiful wedding. Now I just wanted to proclaim my love and devotion to him and actually sign a marriage license myself. And hear him pledge his love and loyalty to me until death do us part.

Because of that expertly forged marriage license, there was no way to get legally married now without blowing everything. Including our cover that the marriage had been genuine from the beginning and I'd been the girl who'd said "I do."

We could have a recommitment ceremony at any time. Or a religious ceremony to augment the quickie Reno wedding Jus had had. But we couldn't get a second marriage certificate that we'd both actually, and genuinely, signed. Not unless we divorced and remarried. Otherwise, we'd be committing perjury, as far as the state knew, when we vowed that neither of us was currently married. And the new marriage still wouldn't be legal.

And a divorce? Imagine the scandal! How would we explain it? And the legal mess it would create! I shuddered at the thought.

Both the local Seattle and national media watched everything Jus did. Before he'd "married" me, he'd been one of Seattle's hottest bachelors, the cute, nerdy one. The billionaire every girl wanted. If I divorced him for two seconds the fortune hunters would circle and the rumors would fly. No, divorce and remarriage were out as a viable option. If only there were a way to make the marriage happen. Wouldn't that be the perfect Christmas present?

And speaking of Christmas, we were stuck in the middle of a holiday tug-of-war between the parents. Having both sets in the same area complicated things. We'd just had two Thanksgiving meals, if you could call them that. Now the parents were fighting over who got us for Christmas Day and who got Christmas Eve. Or would both days be split evenly between families?

As was tradition for his parents, they were heading out to the Bahamas late Christmas Day to run yet another rugby tournament. They owned and ran a company that ran tournaments and camps during summer and holidays for high school and college rugby players worldwide. So they, naturally, wanted us on Christmas Eve. Even though they were staunch open-presents-Christmas-morning people. Their plan was for us to drop by my parents for dinner and then come spend the night with them.

My parents opened presents Christmas Eve, got up to Christmas socks Christmas morning, then had the extended family over for brunch. So, conflict. Sigh. And, of course, everything was predicated on my dad not getting called to an emergency.

The doorbell rang. Ah! There was my delivery guy. I smiled at the thought of Jus getting his present.

CHAPTER TWO

Kayla

At noon, I met my friend Kelly in Bellevue for lunch. She was one of my few friends who wasn't in retail and slammed with peak. Kelly and I were sorority sisters in college. She'd been the president of the house my senior year. She worked in Bellevue not too far from our penthouse. If Jus and I had still been living there I could have walked to lunch.

I arrived at the wine bar and café just a few minutes late. Kelly was her usual self. Still thin and beautifully poised and confident. She was seated at a table near the window, waiting for me. She waved and popped to her feet when she spotted me come in. We teepee hugged because of my baby bump.

"You look fantastic!" Her gaze fell to my stomach.

"Liar!" I laughed. "You're the one who looks great, as always. I feel like a beached whale."

"Do you? You don't look it." She shook her head, with a twinkle in her eyes. "You *look* more like you swallowed a beach ball than whale-like at all.

I laughed. As I sat, my stomach bumped the table. "I'm clumsy, too! My body keeps forgetting how much it sticks out in front now. It still thinks I'm skinny and misjudges distances. Like how far I should pull out my chair. The correct answer? Into the next room!" I shook my head at myself. "You should see the small spaces I've tried to squeeze through and failed."

Kelly grinned as she pulled in her chair and sat. "You may feel big, but you *look* great. From the back, you can't even tell you're pregnant. It's only when you turn around, and then, wow! Stomach." She put her napkin on her lap. "So. How's life with Justin?"

Kelly had known Jus when we were in college, too. He used to hang around the sorority house when I would let him. At the time, I'd been dating Eric, a hot, popular frat guy. Kelly had been as stunned as everyone else when Eric and I broke up and Jus and I married suddenly.

"You mean without Jus?" The baby kicked, taking my breath away. I winced.

Kelly's mouth fell open. She got that embarrassed look people get when they think they've just stepped in it.

"Oh, not like that!" I hoped no one else had overheard and gotten the wrong idea, too. If they had, it would be all over the news by six.

"We're fine," I said a little too loudly. Which came off sounding desperate. Completely opposite of what I wanted.

"And, by the way, don't ever believe the tabloids. They're always claiming to have the scoop on our breakup." I laughed, trying to appear casual and carefree, and explained about peak.

"I haven't seen Jus since Thursday afternoon. I'm eternally grateful to you for distracting me from Cyber Monday. With any luck, he'll be home in the wee hours of the morning tonight."

I paused. "That doesn't make any sense, does it?" I laughed again. "He'll be home in the early hours of tomorrow morning? Late tonight? After midnight when Cyber Monday officially becomes Tuesday?" I sighed. "Something like that, anyway."

We ordered and, over lunch, quickly fell into catching up and sharing gossip we'd heard about mutual friends and our fellow sorority sisters.

When we'd nearly finished our meal, Kelly leaned forward, her eyes lit with mischief and gossip.

I knew that look. She was about to spill something juicy.

"Have you heard the latest about Victoria?"

"No." I leaned forward, too, eager for something salacious. "What has Vicki been up to?"

Vicki was always up to something. She was unconventional, for a Double Deltsie, and adventurous. That's what everyone liked and admired about her.

"Can you keep a secret?" Kelly looked at me slyly over the remains of her meal.

Could I keep a secret? She was talking to the queen of secrets.

"You know I can. My lips are sealed. I swear on my Double Deltsie pin not to tell anyone."

She grinned. "Just pulling your chain. I know you're as good as your word." She lowered her voice. "She had a secret marriage!"

"A secret marriage? What?" My pulse roared in my ears. Or maybe that was just the coffee grinder someone behind the counter had geared up. Anyway, evidently, there were a rash of secret marriages this year. But I wasn't about to tell Kelly the truth of mine.

"What do you mean?" I said. "Isn't she engaged to Joe? Did she dump him and marry someone else without anyone knowing?"

Victoria had been living with Joe for over a year. Nice guy. Not terribly ambitious. I hadn't seen anything about a breakup or her marriage on any of my social media. But if the marriage were secret, I wouldn't hear about it, would I?

Kelly nodded. "Yes, Joe. Who else?"

"But why in secret?" I was confused. "What about her wedding plans for next summer? I already have the save-the-date card."

"Exactly." Kelly did the bobblehead thing. "And that's the problem. Joe lost his job in May, and with it, his health insurance. No biggie, right? But you have to have insurance or get fined. And health insurance is expensive. Especially when you don't have a job.

"So, you know, Victoria. She's pragmatic and likes to flaunt the rules."

Which was ironic for someone who had been head of our sorority standards board for over a year. The standards board members were the cops of the house, policing policy violations, and acting as judge and jury when an offending member came before them.

But, as Vicki told me when I expressed shock she was running for the job the first time, if she was head of the board, she could bend the rules to suit *her* interpretation and spare her friends. She could be the benevolent dictator of the house.

When she was elected by a landslide, her board became a kind of supreme court that didn't care much for the letter of the law. She was known for turning a blind eye to anything that wasn't completely egregious and blatantly thrown in her face. Her motto had been "I don't care what you do as long as I don't know about it."

"She and Joe already put nonrefundable deposits down on their venue and catering, so they couldn't move up the wedding date," Kelly said as she sat back in her chair. "Her mom would kill her.

"So they decided to quietly go to the courthouse and get married in a civil ceremony so Joe could go on her health plan immediately. They thought it would be no problem to have the religious ceremony for her family and friends next summer. No one would be the wiser."

I shrugged, disappointed in Victoria's so-called scandal. It wasn't nearly as brash and unconventional as mine.

"What's scandalous about that?" I said. "It sounds like good common sense."

"It was. But, like I said, she didn't tell her parents because her mom would flip. But not a problem. Why would her mom have to know?

"Until her mom started insisting she be the one to turn the license in to the state to register the marriage. Suddenly, Vicki needs a second license. *Badly.* And finds out she can't get a second license in Washington State. It's illegal when you're already married."

Tell me about it! Nothing new there. I frowned. Vicki's problem seemed minor compared to mine.

"Turning in the license to register the marriage with the state is the pastor's job." I'd been a maid of honor enough times to know that. "Why doesn't she just tell her mom that?"

"Because of her older sister." Kelly looked smug. She'd come to the main point now. "Her sister had a big wedding ceremony three years ago. Threw the bouquet. Stuffed cake in her groom's mouth. Went on the honeymoon." Kelly paused. "Here's the kicker—she never signed the license. Or turned it in. Disappeared for a while after the ceremony with the groom so it would *look* like she was doing the signing. Faked everyone out. But it was all a hoax."

Crap. I knew about hoaxes, all too well.

"She 'got married' just to please her parents," Kelly said. "Now Vicki's mom doesn't trust *Vicki.* Like dishonesty is somehow genetic and she's predestined to pull the same trick. If Vicki's mom is going to pay for a big ceremony again this time, she wants to make sure it's actually a legal marriage, not a fake."

"Wow," I said, warming to the magnitude of the scandal. "*Audacious.*"

Kelly nodded. "And unfortunate for Victoria. Vicki and Joe can't afford a big wedding on their own. A rational adult would simply tell a rational set of parents her very logical reason for doing what she did. Because she loves Joe, she wants him covered in case he gets sick. But that isn't going to fly with her family. Not after what her sister did."

Okay. So Victoria's problems were beginning to look similar to mine. But at least she'd really married her guy.

"Now she's scrambling to find some way to get a legal second license her mom can file. She's done a ton of research." Kelly paused, giving gravity to the situation. "It's an obscure issue. Only New York State will allow and issue a legal second license. *If* the authority performing the ceremony demands it.

"Unfortunately for Victoria, you have to get married in New York to use it. Which is out. Her venue is here in Washington."

My heart stopped. I almost choked on my coffee. Kelly kept talking but I didn't hear what she was saying. My mind was whirling.

Kelly frowned. "Kayla? Are you okay?"

I nodded and took a sip of water. "I choke easily these day. New York, did you say?"

She nodded. "Yeah, if you know the right search terms to use, you can Google it. Try secret wedding. That's how she found it. There are forums that discuss secret weddings, believe it or not."

Why hadn't I thought of that? Suddenly, I was grinning. *Jus, I just found your Christmas present. And mine, too. A secret New York second—or first, as our case may be—wedding. What could be more perfect?*

CHAPTER THREE

Kayla

As we parted, I hugged Kelly goodbye with more enthusiasm than she expected. Little did she know she'd
just solved a major problem for Jus and me. *Merry
Christmas, Kayla and Jus!*

I played Christmas music all the way home, listening
to songs extolling the virtues of love, faith, and loyalty
making great gifts. Didn't I know it! That was what I
was aiming for.

By the time I walked in the door of home, I was as
ebullient as a round, jolly, old elf like Saint Nick. I
hummed the latest in Christmas music and practically
danced my way into the entry. The scent of fresh fir
trees perfumed the air, along with a faint hint of cin-

namon and ginger, giving a real feeling of Christmas to the place. Magda had probably been baking earlier.

It was only a little after three, but Magda had gone for the day. She'd left me a note and dinner in the fridge, with instructions on how to heat it up. These solo dinners were getting monotonous. It was no use texting Jus to see if he'd be home for dinner. He wouldn't.

I frowned. No text from him, either. I hoped he'd gotten my advent calendar delivery.

Oh, well. Nothing dimmed my good cheer. In fact, for the moment, I relished my time alone. Now I had plenty of time to plan my surprise wedding. I pulled off my coat and boots, hung my coat in the closet, and padded off to my office to begin my research.

Outside, the clouds had cleared and the sun was peeking out, low in the sky. The sun set before five now. It was threatening a beautiful sunset. My office faced west, like the kitchen and as much of the house as could possibly manage it. Most of the west side of the house was view windows. The views were all to the west across the lake. To the east was a hill. So not much of an exciting view there except for the driveway and the gardens. Nice, but not the same as lake, mountains, and cityscape.

My iMac booted up and within minutes I'd found exactly what Kelly had promised—the forums. With links to the New York State official website with all the official rules and regulations for obtaining licenses and getting married. Why hadn't I thought of this earlier?

I guessed I hadn't believed it was possible. And to be fair to Jus and me, like Kelly had said, it was obscure. Only one state in the country allowed for a second license when you were already married. The original mention of the second license was buried in a forum discussing problems with secret weddings and in-laws.

There was only a scant paragraph about it on the official New York State website, as if it were an afterthought by some overworked official. A situation that pertained to only a few, niche marriage situations unlikely to be of interest to the general marrying public. But to those of us who needed it, it was gold.

Jus and my relationship had evolved. Maybe it was like boiling a frog, that's why we hadn't tumbled to this solution. We'd just slowly gotten used to faking the marriage. We'd been too busy with a million other high-priority things to give it much thought.

Our marriage started out as a business contract that was scheduled to end in divorce at the one-year mark. Jus had promised me a ten-million-dollar payout for my trouble. Before our expiration date, long before, we fell in love. And hit more than a few snags before we both admitted our love for each other and decided to stay together and turn this fake marriage into the genuine thing.

And then peak hit with a vengeance. And Jus got distracted. And why sweat it, anyway? To our family and friends, and most importantly, in the eyes of the state, we *were* legally married.

And now here I was, with the perfect present dumped into my lap as I listened to Christmas music and my heart filled with joy.

If I hadn't had lunch with Kelly, my marriage to Jus might have stayed the way it was—instituted by an imposter, faked for the rest of our lives by us. At least I'd learned a lesson—challenge your assumptions from time to time. Think outside the box. And never be satisfied when the status quo could be better.

When I was excited, I had the tendency to be impatient and energetic. I could barely stay in my chair. I kept wanting to bounce out. My eyes skimmed the page. Partly as a protection mechanism. I didn't want to find anything in the rules and regulations for New York that would upset the happy wedding plans dancing in my head like sugarplums.

I had to force my eyes to stop racing down the screen. All that stupid training in elementary school to read faster was a nuisance at times. I took a deep breath, trying to calm my heart. *Take it slow and easy, girl. One word at a time.*

Here were the pertinent rules:

We did not have to be a resident of New York State to be married there! *Thank goodness for that. I didn't have time to establish residency, and I could just imagine the questioning I would get from Jus if I suggested buying, or renting, another house, one in New York.*

We needed both a photo ID (driver's license or passport) and a proof of age (birth certificate). *No problem there.*

Both of us had to appear at the office of the town or city clerk in person, together, and at the same time. *That could be arranged.*

There was a twenty-four-hour waiting period after applying. *Okay, a few days of vacation time in New York! Which meant we'd have to do this after the first of the year and peak was over. Jus had half of Christmas Eve off and Christmas Day. Theoretically, anyway. In reality? Eh. He'd be back in the office preparing for the day after as soon as dinner was over and his parents were on their plane for the Bahamas.*

I was six months pregnant, so I still had a couple of months before I got into the no-fly zone. It would have been romantic to get married on Valentine's Day. That way, we could buy each other presents and cards and celebrate our love with no one catching on we were really celebrating our genuine anniversary. But that was pushing things a little late. If we got married by the end of January, we would be fine.

If we had to marry before the twenty-four-hour waiting period was over, we could request a judicial waiver from the county clerk in the county (borough) where we obtained our marriage license. *That shouldn't be necessary.*

No blood test or physical exam required.

No proxy marriages. But you could marry your cousin. *What?*

The license was valid for sixty days and could be used anywhere within New York State. But not outside its bounds.

I forced myself to keep reading, holding my breath when I came to the heading for witnesses. Many states, like Washington, required two...

But New York required only one! Way to go New York. Whew!

Only two other people in the world knew the truth about our marriage—my cousin Dex and our lawyer Harry Lawrence. Dex was finishing his master's degree in some tech geeky thing across the state. I could bribe him to be our witness with a private jet trip to New York for a weekend and the promise of an adventure. And cold, hard cash if necessary. And Harry could work any legal angles that needed ironing out. Perfect!

And here was the key point—for a second or subsequent ceremony, the officiant (what a pompous, governmental word) of the subsequent ceremony may require a license be presented before performing the ceremony. In that case, a couple already legally married may apply for a second or subsequent license. As is the case with the first ceremony, the issuing town or city will once again issue a Certificate of Marriage Registration.

Dance of joy, dance of joy, dance of joy!

All I had to do was find an officiant who would require a license and the perfect private winter wedding would be ours. How hard could that be?

Justin

I hadn't been home since Thanksgiving. I'd been sleeping on the sofa in my office and showering at the gym down the street like I was still cramming for exams in college. I was bleary from sleep exhaustion and elated from the success of the day. Living on borrowed adrenaline.

I hadn't had sex in four days. I was horny as hell. I missed Kay. I was ready for Kay. I tried not to think about it too hard. Things were hard enough as it was.

I pulled into the garage at two a.m. and slid silently into the house. It had been transformed for Christmas. I felt like I'd been gone forever. The seasons had changed during my absence. The decorative pumpkins, leaves, and fowl of various sorts were gone. All the brown, yellow, and orange replaced with red and green in rich fabrics and expensive crystal ornaments.

Inside smelled like the holidays—spices and fir. With my eyes used to the dark, I didn't turn on the lights. I stood at the bottom of the stairs taking in the fresh garland that wound up the banister and the tall tree in the living room that sparkled in the moonlight slanting in.

I should have fallen asleep on my feet. This must have been how zombies felt. If zombies got horny. I'd barely had eight hours' sleep in four days. But I was high and eager.

We'd done it. Cyber Monday had been killer. We'd taken a larger share of the pie away from our competitors, major, established department stores and chains, than we had last year. Early results indicated we'd made record profits, too. Storms were brewing on the horizon. Business hurdles I hoped we didn't have to jump. But we were in the black, which should make our investors happy. A boost in our stock evaluation would make my Christmas.

I kicked off my shoes and bounded up the stairs toward the master bedroom, carrying a bag with a surprise for Kay. By the time I reached the top of the stairs, I was hot for her and ready to go.

I sneaked into the bedroom and set the bag on my nightstand. Kay was sound asleep on her left side, snuggled into her pregnancy sleep pillow the way she used to curl up around me.

Shit. I'd been replaced by a pillow. Except that damn pillow didn't have a hard-on for her and know how to please her.

I stripped out of my clothes and slid in beneath the covers behind her, sliding my dick between her legs as I caressed her shoulder.

"Babe?" I whispered. I'd been hoping for a more enthusiastic greeting. Like Kay actually waking up.

She sighed softly, so sexily my heart pounded as she stirred.

There was something about her being pregnant with my baby that made her incredibly hot. My virility and masculinity on display.

I put that baby in her. For a geek like me, that was saying something. I couldn't believe this beautiful woman let me touch her, let alone have sex with her.

Seeing her big with my baby brought out all my protective urges. Kay and my baby were everything to me.

My fingers itched to touch her. Since getting pregnant, her beautiful breasts had become fuller. I slid my hand beneath her nightgown. When I cupped her breast, the nipple budded up, long and hard like it had missed me. I'd sure missed it.

Her lips parted. She sighed softly and backed into me.

I pulled her panties down and slid my fingers between her legs. Her breasts weren't the only things that had gotten large with pregnancy. Kay was moist and ready for me. I wasn't going to hold on long.

I slid my fingers inside her and breathed in her ear. "I'm home, baby. Miss me? I missed you. I need you."

Kayla

I was in the middle of a white mist and gently falling snow, thin, and lithe. Dancing in toe shoes in a flowing white dress as stars tried to twinkle through the fog. Like Clara in *The Nutcracker*. Snow that wasn't cold. Just soft and sparkling.

Arms wrapped around me from behind. Strong, warm, insistent arms that came from out of nowhere. A man nuzzled my neck from behind. I brushed him away, but he held on and kissed my neck.

"I'm home, baby. Miss me?" His voice was deep and sexy. His fur collar tickled my neck.

Miss him? I didn't even know him. But that voice...his voice was familiar, like I *should* know it. Maybe he was my nutcracker.

When he lifted my dress and slid between my legs, I barely struggled.

"Baby." It was almost a groan of sexual pleasure as he cupped my breast.

I should push him away. But I didn't want to. I laughed and grabbed the hand that held my breast.

"It's me, Kay. Wake up. One way or another, I'm making love to you."

Still in the clutches of my dream world, I looked over my shoulder. "Jus?"

He wore a tall hat and boots. And I knew I was dreaming because Jus would never dress like that, like a soldier out of the Victorian era.

I didn't want to wake up. I wanted to stay in that dream state where a dream lover with a real dick was just the thing. At the same time, Jus was home and I was happy.

Even though I always fought being pulled from sleep, I loved it when he came to bed and made love to me when I was still dreamy. When I was in that twilight state, his lovemaking had the added intensity of the erotic sensations of a dream. Those emotions you can't name, only feel. Since getting pregnant my hormones ran high; every sexual touch was magnified. I was hungry for his.

I backed into him, eyes closed, letting myself feel every inch of him, and take in his scent and heat while the white mist blended into the moonlight coming in through the half-shut blinds of our room.

Maybe it wasn't all pregnancy. Maybe it was the strength of my love and passion for Jus, too.

He lifted the hair off the back of my neck and sucked on my neck, his tongue doing a twirl that sent a shiver of pleasure through me. His breath was hot in my ear. Since September, he'd grown his beard back.

At my insistence. It was rough and soft at the same time against my skin, the fur collar of my dream.

He trailed kisses down my shoulder, his mouth warm and moist. I shivered with delight and need.

My skin had grown increasingly sensitive since I got pregnant. Excess estrogen. Lovely extra estrogen that made my breasts ache for his touch and my clit reach for his fingers.

"Stop teasing me with your fingers and give me the real thing. Slide inside where I need you, Jus."

He took my chin and turned my face to his, kissing me tenderly and deeply.

I kissed him back and pulled up my nightgown, pulled it over my head, and dropped it over the edge of the bed to the floor.

I opened my eyes just a crack and stole a glimpse of him over my shoulder. He was silhouetted in the moonlight coming through the upper window of our master suite. He had a look of wonder and desire on his face. He was delightfully naked and aroused as he slid between my legs and rubbed against me. Just the way I liked him.

Everything was still dreamlike. I fought full wakefulness. I wanted him to make love to me in that space between dream and reality. I backed into him, positioning him at my opening. "Do it, Jus. Do it *now*. I'm so ready for you."

He playfully bit my shoulder and slid in. I shuddered with the first thrust, already on the edge of pleasure. My extra hormones made me bloom for him. I came quickly these days.

We were both needy. Both ready. Both almost breathless with desire. I closed my eyes and let the dreamlike state carry me as I rocked into him behind me. It only took a couple of thrusts to throw me over the edge into wave after wave of climax.

I gasped and called out his name. Everything was so intense with him. I squeezed him as he stiffened behind me and gave a final thrust.

When it was over, he held me tight and cradled me tenderly. My uterus contracted with my climax and became hard and tight. I had to breathe through it, unable to speak.

"I love you, Kay. I missed you."

"I love you, too." I was truly breathless. "You take my breath away." I gasped as the baby kicked. "Baby kick. She gets jealous when her parents have sex."

I moved his hand so he could feel it. In reality, I didn't think she liked having her living quarters cramped and contracted.

I felt Jus smile against my back.

He kissed the back of my head. "She's a little tyrant." He rubbed my baby bump, trying to calm her. "Nice muscles."

"Cyber Monday?" I said, drowsy and sated.

"A huge success."

Justin

I slept like the dead and got up early the next morning. I was showering in the glass-encased shower, enjoying the steam and the feel of hot water waking me, when I noticed the bathroom door to the bedroom was open a crack. And Kay's eye was peeking through.

I turned toward the door, grabbed my dick, and gave it a good stroke or two for her benefit.

She laughed as she opened the door and stepped in, carrying the bag I'd left on my nightstand.

"Are you spying on me?" I didn't know why that made me so happy. Maybe because all the time I was growing up, no girl had looked at my scrawny, nerdy self twice. The thought of seeing me naked would have sent any reasonable girl with half-decent eyesight running, not panting with lust. Now this beautiful blond was playing voyeur to get an eyeful.

"Just seeing whether you're being naughty or nice." Her eyes danced.

"I can be *very* naughty." I opened the shower door and reached for her, grabbing her by the wrist, ready to pull her in, nightgown and all. Water ran down my face and dripped off my beard.

She laughed and rattled the bag. "What's this?"

"Yesterday was the first day of advent. That's your first chocolate."

"Copycat! It's late," she said with a flirt in her voice as she wrenched free of my grip.

"Copycat?" I frowned, confused.

"Didn't you get the advent calendar I had delivered to you yesterday?" She took a step back, out of reach.

Water was dripping on the floor. I closed the shower and thought for a minute, before it dawned on me. "I got a lot of packages yesterday. The suppliers have begun their annual onslaught of thank-you gifts. I didn't have time to open any. I had Danielle set them aside. It's probably in with those."

She shook her head, looking incredibly, sexily disappointed. "So much for the element of surprise."

"Great minds think alike," I said. "I'll open it first thing today when I get to the office."

"You better. You have two days of surprises waiting for you." She pulled the single-chocolate box out of the bag and opened it.

I loved watching her as her eyes went wide.

"It's an angel covered in gold flake." She looked at me. "It's beautiful." Her eyes were misty and soft.

"Her mouth was like a jewel as she feasted on twenty-four-karat gold." I nodded toward it and brushed my wet hair back.

"It's too beautiful to eat."

"It's too decadent and tasty not to. If you don't eat it, you'll never know what you're missing."

She got a devilish look in her eyes. "Is this like a chocolate Santa? Do you eat the head or the feet of an angel first?"

"The wings." I grinned. "So it can't fly away."

I watched her reaction closely as she took it out of its box and set the bag and the box on the counter. She closed her eyes and arched her neck as she tasted it, looking rapturous. "Dark chocolate, raspberry, and gold. This is the best thing I've ever tasted."

She walked over to me. "You have to try this." She put it between her lips, leaving some sticking out for me, and opened the shower door so I could have a taste.

I pulled her into my arms, pressing her against my wet body as I kissed her and stole half her chocolate. Before she could protest, I pulled her into the shower.

"I'm still dressed!" She was laughing in the steam as the shower soaked her white nightgown.

I pulled her nightgown off and dropped it outside the shower, giving her a triumphant look. Then I sat her on the bench of the shower and made love to her.

"Naughty enough for you?" I said when we were finished.

"Nothing but coal in your stocking this year. You're going to have to be *very* good the rest of the year to make up for it." She laughed. "You're simply insatiable."

She kissed me, grabbed the towel I'd slung over the shower door, and slid out of the shower, leaving me alone and towel-less. "And I have to pee."

"You always have to pee. Hey, come back with my towel!"

"No time. Your baby is dancing on my bladder."

"My baby now?" I arched a brow.

She laughed. "Tap dancing, no less."

Laughing, she disappeared into the room with the toilet and closed the door.

I wanted to give Kay everything. I loved her that much. She wasn't complaining, but I knew she'd been disappointed by Thanksgiving and how much I worked over the holiday weekend. I was touched that she'd sent me an advent calendar. And embarrassed that I'd been a douchebag and not made time to open it. She was magnanimous and forgiving about that, too.

I remembered Kay in college, and how she'd loved the holidays. She'd planned the decorations for her sorority and almost singlehandedly ran the Christmas party, including the secret elves program. She'd been almost giddy with the fun of it. Which was why I'd put her in charge of the employees' Santa Sample Sale. She was already in charge of the majority of our charitable donations and organizations. But I wanted her to have an active hand in managing the sample sale. If she was up to it.

I hoped it made her happy. This was the first holiday season we'd spent together and I was already blowing them with my workaholic tendencies. For me, the holidays were like tax season to an accountant. Fourteen-hour days or more and little sleep. I'd known this going in. But I'd dragged Kay in unaware.

There was nothing I could do about it. In retail, this was make-it-or-break-it time. I had to work hard to keep Flash going.

That left Kay to deal with holiday stress. Our parents were the primary source of it. Each set vying for an extra minute with us.

I wanted to give Kay something special for Christmas. You would think being a billionaire would have made that easy. Ironically, it made it more difficult. It was too easy to buy something expensive and pass it off as thoughtful. Kay would see right through something an empty gesture.

Yes, I worked hard for what we had. But now that I could afford almost anything, it made things somehow less meaningful.

I was determined to do something memorable. To make up for being an absentee husband for a few months. During some of those hours when I was drinking too many energy drinks and too much coffee, and showering at the gym, I'd been struck with an idea— family peace. It may not have been as profound as world peace. But it was a good start.

If I could take the stress off Kay by setting a precedent of how we'd deal with family and holidays, I would be banking holiday capital for the rest of our lives. If I could start a tradition that was uniquely ours that we could carry on throughout the years, wouldn't that be worth doing? Some time that we'd set apart for family, but wouldn't consume us. Something we could eventually bring children to. Like next year. Wow. My kid would be nine months old next year.

In that vein, I'd peppered Kay's friends Britt and Sarah, who both worked for me at Flash, with questions about what would thrill Kay most, tradition-wise. I had several restrictions on it. It had to be something here in Seattle. Something that we could do in the afternoon or evening of Christmas Eve that could involve both families. And, eventually, children. Something that said Christmas. Something classic. Something with staying power.

Britt, who knew Kay better than anybody, had come up with the answer. Give that girl a bonus!

"Kayla loves *The Nutcracker* ballet. But I think she only got to go once or twice as a girl. And one of those times was with my family. We got all dressed up in twin velvet dresses. It was so much fun. Kayla said she'd love to do it every year. She just loves all the dancing and the music." Britt raised her eyebrows as she looked at me for verification.

"The ballet?" I wasn't convinced.

Britt rolled her eyes. "Men! You don't get it. It's a Christmas story and a romance. Women love it. Kids love it. Even little boys love it. I mean, the Nutcracker fights the rats!" She continued staring at me.

I was thinking.

"They retired the Maurice Sendak sets after last year's season," Britt said. "This year the sets are brand new, designed by children's author Ian Falconer. And they've returned to George Balanchine's 1954 choreography." Britt nodded. "The Maurice Sendak sets lasted thirty years. This could be the start of something big."

Ballet? Not my thing. Not my dad's thing. Or my two brothers'. Mom might like it. Kay's parents? I had no idea. But if Kay would love it, I would do it. I could sit through a few hours of ballet for her sake. To make everything up to her for missing the holiday action and leaving the holiday burdens to her.

Getting tickets, however, especially for Christmas Eve, had been challenging. The show sold out in October. Getting eight seats together? Practically impossible. I put my talented new assistant Danielle on it.

It took some doing. Some finagling. And the negotiation skills of our chief procurement officer in addition to Danielle. We had to call in more than a few favors. Finally, one of Riggins' friends agreed to trade a week at his ski chalet at Whistler over New Year's for one of the board members for the children's hospital eight-seat box at the ballet. I agreed to be a sponsor at Riggins' friend's annual golf tournament for charity. And over a handshake, the deal was done.

Then I'd booked dinner reservations after the show at one of Seattle's top steakhouses, to make it up to Dad and my brothers for the ballet. And now all that was left was to give Kay the exciting news—family problems solved. We'd all spend Christmas Eve together at the brand new *Nutcracker* and have Christmas Eve dinner no one would have to cook.

We'd open presents and spend the night at Kay's parents. Go to mine for breakfast. See them off. And have dinner with Kay's. In the meantime, Danielle had gotten me on the list for season tickets for the ballet for next year so the tradition could continue. Now all that was left was to surprise Kay with it.

I'd also picked out a little something special for Kay to wear to the ballet.

I was happy just thinking how happy Kay would be when I surprised her with the tickets. First, I had to get buy-in from both sets of parents.

CHAPTER FOUR

Tuesday, December 2nd
Kayla
I was at the breakfast table, eating a cranberry scone,
when Jus joined me. Magda, certain he wasn't eating
right at work, had made him a plate of scrambled eggs
and sausage. I tried not to look at it. I was at the end of
my second trimester and rarely had morning sickness
now, but something about eggs didn't sit right with
me.

He flashed me a knowing, intimate look that would
have made me laugh if Magda hadn't been watching.
He was carrying a small, wrapped present. He slid it
across the table to me as he sat.

"What's this?" I asked as I took it from him.

Magda poured him a cup of coffee.

"December 2nd, second day of advent." He nodded to it as he took a sip of his coffee, a dark, aromatic African bean Christmas blend I'd gone specifically to the roastery to get. It was a roastery exclusive, and worth the trip.

"Open it," he said, indicating the present.

I pulled the ribbon off. Inside was a box from my favorite jewelry store. I lifted the lid to reveal a gold charm bracelet with a single snowflake bead decorated with crystals. At least, I *thought* they were crystals. With Jus, you never knew. They could have been diamonds. I had a pretty good eye for diamonds, but a good crystal could sometimes fake me out. I sensed a theme.

"It's just crystal," he said, as if reading my mind.

"It's beautiful." I had an idea that by Christmas the bracelet would be filled with holiday-themed beads. I leaned across the table to kiss him. And bumped it, of course, rattling our glasses.

"Your ob appointment's today, isn't it?" he said.

"Sweet of you to remember."

He laughed. "I have it in my calendar. Do you want me to be there?"

I had a moment of panic. He'd been very supportive, not missing an appointment when he was in town. Even going so far as to try to schedule his trips around them when he could. But I wanted to talk to my doctor about my travel plans. I didn't want Jus around for that.

I shook my head. "No, you're busy. And this is just a quick, routine visit. No ultrasounds. Nothing special going on. There's no need for you to waste a couple of hours of prime work time for a five-minute appointment."

He looked relieved.

"I'd rather have you home early for dinner." I was pulling his chain again. I knew he wouldn't be home for dinner, let alone early. But I said it with a straight face so I could enjoy his reaction. Yes, I was an evil woman. One tick against my name on Santa's list.

His face fell. He looked contrite and apologetic. I watched Jus the politician and negotiator come out. "Kay—"

I laughed. "Don't worry. I'm teasing. I'd rather you get done what you need to. I'll text you after the appointment." I paused. "But, seriously, will you be home sometime tonight?"

"I hope so." He looked sheepish.

After Jus left for work, I wandered to our bedroom to shower for my doctor's appointment. I had a ton of work to do to get the sample sale ready and plan the parties. I needed to meet with Britt and the other merchandise buyers to see what samples they had to contribute to the sale.

Flash ran a sample sale for the employees about once a month to every six weeks throughout the year. Once a year they held a public sale. And once a year they held one specifically for the employees and supporters of the local children's hospital. The employee sales were always held in a big conference room on the ground floor of the Flash office building and looked a lot like a garage sale. Stuff strewn everywhere. Employees grabbing for the best finds.

Things were ridiculously cheap at the sales, pennies on the dollar. All the items were donated by the manufacturers who didn't want their samples back after Flash had either used them to determine which items to feature or had photographed them for the catalogue. Often it was more expensive to send the samples back than for the manufacturer to donate them.

All the proceeds from the sales went to the children's hospital as a charitable donation. Members of the children's hospital charitable organization manned the sales, acting as clerks and helping set up and tear down.

Since the big charity sample sale in September, I'd been in close contact with the merch buyers. They were under strict instructions to hold back the best deals for December sale. And lock them in a top-secret storage unit at the office. I'd nicknamed it Santa's closet.

I'd also instituted a holiday wish box where employees could drop in suggestions for items they were wishing would show up at the sale. Employees were some of Flash's best customers. They watched the website with keen eyes for bargains. The suggestions came streaming in. The merch buyers were supposed to be holding samples that matched wishes for the December sale. I had actually set up a simple inventory management system to keep track of what we had.

I wanted it to be the best sale ever, a real Christmas wish come true for hardworking people who didn't always have a lot of extra money to spend. Jus and Riggins paid their employees the most they could, but they had to stay competitive. Many employees certainly had no time during the holidays to shop, other than online.

In just the few short years Flash had been in business, the Santa Sample Sale had become a tradition. A sort of Santa's Secret Shop for grownups where employees could pick up last-minute gifts and surprises for their friends and family. Jus said it was great fun for the employees. Riding high from the success of the September sample sale charity event I'd run, I planned to make this holiday sale the best one yet.

It would be almost like Flash was playing Santa to its employees. What a happy thought. Christmas morning with its socks full of surprises was one of my favorite parts of the holiday. And this would be a little bit like it.

I was filled with happy thoughts as I stripped down for the shower. So much so that I wasn't paying attention to either my body or my clothes as I turned the water on and waited for our tankless water heater to get a nice head of steam going. It wasn't until I stepped into the shower that I noticed a tiny trail of pink swirling in the water at my feet.

My heart stopped for a minute. I was spotting.

Justin

First thing when I got to the office, I opened the calendar from Kay. It was from the coffee company that had a branch in our office complex. I opened the red tin for December 1st. A small package of chocolate-covered espresso beans and a coupon for a fifteen-minute relaxation message from a travelling masseuse. Just what I needed.

I held off opening today's tin. Something to look forward to later, kind of like Christmas.

I'd just settled in to look over the morning reports when there was a knock on my door.

Paul Conner, my chief procurement officer, poked his head in. "Gotta minute?" He was frowning.

Not a good sign.

I waved him in.

He closed the door behind him. "We have a problem. I just heard from my brother-in-law on the port commission. The longshoreman rejected their contract. They voted to strike. We have a matter of hours before every port on the West Coast shuts down. It will be all over the news before noon."

"Shit." I thumped back in my chair and tried to breathe.

Paul nodded. "The longshoremen may have just stopped Christmas from coming. At least for us."

I cursed beneath my breath and shook my head. "We're not cancelling Christmas."

Without the port, how the hell were we going to get all our goods from overseas? Rumors of a possible strike had been flying all fall as the negotiations dragged on. Everyone had been hoping it wouldn't come to this. Damn.

I grabbed my phone and sent out a high-priority text to Riggins, our top execs and senior managers, and, most importantly, the head of transportation.

Then I turned my attention to Paul. "How are we set for boxes and bags? We made contingency plans, right?"

"We're set," Paul said. "We have enough packing supplies to box, bag, and mail everything we have on hand and meet all our forecasts. Packaging materials won't be what delay orders. Content is another story."

"There has to be a way through this." I jumped out of my chair. "Where's Darren? We need his transportation team. We have to get somebody to the port and get what we can from any of our shipments still waiting to be unloaded. Immediately. I'll go to the pier myself if I have to."

Kayla

I'd been frantically texting and calling Jus all the way to the doctor's office. No response. It wasn't like Jus to be out of touch. Especially if there was an emergency. Which was clear from how many times I'd texted him in a row with a desperate message to call me.

I was scared as I lay on the examining table in my obstetrician's office with my pregnant belly exposed and covered in ultrasound goo. My heart raced like a rabbit's. I kept hoping to see Jus charge in to the rescue. I just wanted to hold his hand and have him tell me everything was going to be okay.

Dr. Valentine had been studying the ultrasound screen with a serious expression. Her shoulders relaxed. She swung the screen around for me to see. "Everything looks great." She broke into a smile.

I let out a sigh of relief.

"Nothing to worry about. See? Your little girl is perfect. And in the perfect position. The placenta is nice and high and firmly attached. There's no sign of placenta previa or miscarriage."

I was mesmerized by the sight of my baby. She turned and looked directly at the camera. Amazing how clear the ultrasound was. She actually looked like a baby. With unique, distinct features and personality. She looked a little bit like Jus and a little like me. I resisted the urge to wave at her. Instead, I grinned, stupidly relieved.

"Have you recently had sex?" Dr. Valentine set the paddle down and wiped my stomach with a towel.

I wasn't usually shy about the question, but I found myself blushing. And feeling guilty. "Yes?" I said, as if I wasn't sure I wanted to admit to the truth.

Dr. Valentine laughed. "What does that mean? You're not sure?"

"No, I'm sure enough. I've had sex. Several times in the last eight hours." Now I was blushing to my toes.

"Well, then, that's probably our culprit." She squeezed my arm reassuringly. "Bleeding during pregnancy is scary and can be a symptom of a serious problem. In some cases, though, like yours this time, it's harmless. Pregnancy hormones caused you to develop more sensitive, and expanded, blood vessels.

"Light bleeding or spotting during this time in your pregnancy, the second and third trimester, can occur because of a combination of those sensitive vessels and interference with the cervix during sex."

"Is this your way of telling me no more sex?" I hated to ask the question. I was already insecure over Jus. And, at the same time, madly desirous of him. If we couldn't have sex...

But I was being selfish. I would do anything for my baby.

Dr. Valentine, who was always reassuring and kind, and often funny, shook her head. "No! Of course not. Having sex is healthy for you and your relationship."

"I feel foolish for rushing here and panicking," I said, still staring at my baby.

Dr. Valentine shook her head. "You shouldn't. Always let me be the judge of whether the cause of your bleeding is serious or not. As they say, better safe than sorry. It's a motto I live by. Would you like another picture of the baby for the family album?"

I nodded.

She handed me another towel so I could wipe up the remaining remnants of the goo and pressed a button to print a picture of the baby for me. "Do you have any travel plans for Christmas?"

"No." I set the towel aside. "I don't think so. Not until after the first of the year. After Jus gets out of the retail hot zone. Then we may take a few days in late January for a winter vacation on the east coast."

Dr. Valentine's forehead creased. "I'm sorry, Kayla. I feel like Scrooge right now. But I'm going to put the breaks on your plans. If you want to travel, go now, before it's too late. I'm putting you on the no-fly list after Christmas."

"What!" I nearly sat straight up. Nearly, only because it wasn't easy to sit straight up, certainly not
quickly, with a big baby bump slowing me down and
blocking progress. "I thought you said the bleeding
isn't serious."

"It's not, in and of itself. I'm more concerned with
your own history. You were a preemie, right?"

"Yes," I said slowly.

"And so was your mom."

"Yes."

She nodded, looking wise and sympathetic. "There's
a strong genetic component to prematurity and preterm labor. Everything looks good and healthy with
your pregnancy now. You measure out right on schedule. But because both your mom, and her mom, went
into preterm labor, you have a good chance of doing so,
too. We just won't know until it happens. If it happens.

"I was going to talk to you about it during your visit
today even before I knew about the bleeding. You have
a few more weeks to get any wanderlust out of your
system. Come December 26th, you're grounded." She
winked at me. "And I won't have you sneaking out of
town by bus, train, stagecoach, or sleigh, either."

CHAPTER FIVE

Kayla

So many people had branded me a gold digger for suddenly marrying Jus on the spur of the moment in Reno. Even though, of course, an imposter had married him, not me. When I got pregnant, it sealed that "she only married him for his money" opinion in everyone's mind. They were simply jealous. It seemed like every girl in Seattle wanted an adorable billionaire like Jus. I was "that little gold digger."

The best way to hang on to a share of a rich guy's fortune for life? Even after a messy divorce? Have his kid and hit him with child support for at least eighteen years. And make sure it was generous.

At first, and maybe still, popular opinion believed our marriage would fail. Many gave us no more than a few weeks to a month. We'd proved them wrong on that point. But anyone who was betting was still spouting the odds were we wouldn't make it past five years and this baby was my insurance for the future.

They didn't know, of course, how close we'd come to calling it quits. Or how we'd originally had a divorce scheduled for our one-year anniversary.

I texted Jus to ignore my earlier, frantic texts and calls, and headed home. Outside may have been dark with gray clouds, and gloomy, but inside Magda had the house lit and cheery. The Christmas trees were lit and the sound of voices on TV in the background. Our little dog, Data, barked happily and ran to greet me. I scooped her up. "Hey, girl."

Magda was in the kitchen. Her eyes lit up when she saw me. She gave me a hesitant look. "Mrs. Kayla? The baby?"

She'd seen my earlier panic and comforted me while I waited to get in to see my doctor.

"We're both fine." I smiled reassuringly. "Nothing serious. I just panicked."

"No. You were cautious. There's a difference."

I smiled, glad to have Magda around. "Something smells delicious."

"Your lunch. I'm making you a nice winter soup and homemade bread. You need to stay strong and healthy for the baby."

She was "watching" TV while she cooked. She was one of those people who liked the sound of voices constantly around her. She wasn't so much paying attention and watching as having the comforting sound in the background.

My head was whirring with wedding thoughts, but I was touched by her thoughtfulness and concern. "Yum. Can't wait. I have some work to do." Actually, I had a wedding to plan. I took my coat off and hung it in the closet. "I'll be in my office until lunch."

I took off my shoes and slipped into some comfy Christmas slipper socks I'd bought the day after Thanksgiving. They were, frankly, ridiculous, but adorable. And kind of sexy in a Christmasy, funky way. They were red and black Mrs. Claus socks, with white printed lace at the toes and a black belt wrapped around the ankle like an anklet. My silly side coming out.

Jus had a matching Mr. Claus pair he refused to wear. You would think someone with zero fashion sense like my husband would have been game for funny slipper socks. But no. *Killjoy.*

Anyway, these were the softest, most comfortable things I'd ever worn. I loved them and my classy, winter white knee-high slipper boots above all else. And alternated between them. But now that it was the holiday season, the Mrs. Claus socks were on extra duty.

I had a lot of thinking and planning to do. I wanted to be married *before* the baby was born. Just the two of us pledging our love and making things legal. A Christmas season wedding. In the snow in New York. Suddenly, it took on a romantic aura.

After the baby arrived, everything would be that much more complicated. And the wedding would have to wait until I'd gotten back into some semblance of shape and would be confident leaving the baby with someone. Getting married was, of course, complicated by having to keep it absolutely secret. I really didn't want a public recommitment ceremony for this. I'd rather do that someplace romantic. If we did it all.

No, I decided as I settled into my office and closed the door. I wouldn't let being grounded after Christmas thwart my plans. Jus had been in such a good mood after his Cyber Monday success. With the business running so smoothly, and safely in the black for the year, it suddenly seemed possible I could talk him into an overnight stay in New York to get married. It would be an *early* Christmas present. So why not?

The thought of a snowy December wedding was suddenly romantic. A real elopement. Yes, terribly romantic. Dex would be done with finals and home from college for Christmas break by the seventeenth. He was the one unromantic aspect of my plans. I loved my cousin, the little geek, but he was a prankster and I didn't want him doing anything to derail the lovely vision I had for my wedding.

A white maternity wedding dress with lace and crystals. A bouquet of white roses and poinsettias. I didn't even need to consult Pinterest for what I had in mind.

I glanced at the calendar on my desk. I would have to work fast. The seventeenth was a Wednesday. We could fly out on the eighteenth. Get our license that afternoon. Get married on the nineteenth...

Or would we have to wait until the twentieth? Damn that twenty-four-hour waiting period. Jus *might* be convinced to slip away for a *few* days, but the fewer, the better chance I had of making my case.

Harry! I snapped my fingers. I would get Harry to get a New York judge to waive the waiting period. I mean, after all, what was the point? We were already "married." For all the State of New York knew we were just two crazy, young, eccentric rich kids who were romantic enough to want to renew their vows at six months.

So, yes! Harry. I grabbed a notepad and scribbled his name to remind me. Harry could certainly convince a judge.

I bit my lip and frowned in thought as I added another note. Make sure Harry gets the marriage record sealed as private so it's not a matter of public record. I didn't want the media getting hold of this news. I shuddered at the thought. They'd make something nasty and scandalous out of it. Claim we were desperate to save our failing marriage. That the vow renewal was a lame attempt to reclaim the magic. Sad, really.

I shrugged off thoughts of gossipy douchebags.

Now all I needed was a little wedding chapel somewhere in snowy upstate New York, a willing officiant—still hated that word—who would require the license, a chartered jet, and a very small bit of Christmas magic to convince Jus, and I was set!

A knock on the door brought me out of my wedding thoughts and back to the real world.

"Mrs. Kayla?"

"Yes?"

Magda cracked the door open and poked her head in. "Lunch is ready."

I nodded and got out of my chair. As I wandered into the kitchen behind Magda, ready to eat at the counter, the news was still on. They cut to the ports and a shot of angry men carrying "On Strike" signs. Fair wages for longshoremen.

A bright blue banner was pegged at the bottom of the screen. *Longshoremen up and down the West Coast on strike. Ports closed for the foreseeable future. Retail giants worried. Will this kill their holiday profits? Wall Street reacts. Retail stocks down on the news.*

My heart thudded to a standstill. My mouth went dry. "Crap."

Magda looked at me, following my gaze to the screen.

So that was why Jus hadn't called or texted me back. All my happy thoughts vanished. All I wanted for Christmas was a real marriage. Enough of this faking things! The port closure had probably just dashed my Christmas wish for a New York wedding.

Justin

I was in meetings, on the phone, scrambling, all day trying to salvage our Christmas orders. We were guaranteeing in-time for Christmas delivery. We were damn well going to make good on it. The Canadian ports were still open. We could ship our goods to Vancouver, B.C., and truck them down or send them by rail. We'd have to deal with customs at the border and incur more costs and time delays. Our East Coast distribution center in Pennsylvania would be fine. The East Coast ports were open. Our Midwest distribution center in Columbus, Ohio, and the one in Reno were in jeopardy.

Flying everything was just too expensive. We'd lose our shirts. Keeping operations running smoothly was going to be dicey from here until long after the strike ended. For every day it went on, shipping containers full of pallets of goods would pile up on the piers. Once the strike ended, it would take days, weeks, or months to get them all unloaded and distributed.

At seven in the evening, my stomach rumbled. I realized I hadn't eaten all day. Or checked personal messages. I wouldn't be going home tonight. I needed to call Kay. I wondered how her doctor appointment had gone. If something had been wrong she would have called me. I was confident of that.

Shit, I thought with a start. I should have thought to check earlier. She'd left me nearly a dozen messages.

When I listened to the first message, my heart stopped. Her voice was panicked and scared. Kay was spotting. We could lose our baby.

I called her before listening to the rest. I was such a crappy husband.

Kayla

I sat out on the covered patio, watching the silent, dark lake and looking at the lights sparkling from the city and homes across from us. A few scattered showers had come through since afternoon.

It was hard for people who weren't Seattleites to understand our relationship with our weather. We had as many names for rain as Finland had for snow. We loved sunshine, but when the rain was gone too long, we felt exposed and nervous. Ready for a comfy rainy day. And yet when it rained again after a long dry spell, it was like Seattle drivers had forgotten how to drive in it. All kinds of accidents.

Seattle in the winter was mostly fifty-five and rainy. And forty to fifty percent or more humidity. Snow for Christmas was a rarity. I'd lived in the Seattle area all my life, except for four years of college, and could only remember a couple of white Christmases. And you had to be generous about what constituted white, as in a dusting that lasted a few hours.

The humidity made it feel colder than it was. Because I was pregnant, I was always warm. It felt good to sit outside on our patio decorated with Christmas lights, sipping hot Christmas blend tea. I wore a light sweater and hadn't bothered to turn the patio heater on. I was perfectly comfortable. Anyone else would have been freezing. But I was enjoying the gentle, cold breeze that was rippling the lake.

Since noon, I'd been plotting. I was determined. Nothing would stop my Christmas wedding. I'd looked it up. We could get a marriage license on Christmas Eve before noon. If Harry could get the twenty-four-hour wait waived, we could be married that afternoon and fly home late Christmas day. Jus could be back in the office first thing on the 26th.

Even Jus wouldn't work on Christmas. If I teased him enough about being Scrooge, I could guilt him in to taking it off. Especially if I promised him he could go into work all the earlier the next day. Ha! *The Christmas Carol.*

It was getting him to take all of Christmas Eve off that worried me. I might have to blow my element of surprise.

My phone sat on the table next to me. It startled me when it sprang to life. Heart pounding, I grabbed it. *Jus.* "Hey, stranger."

"Kay!" He sounded relieved I'd picked up.

Hey, I knew the feeling. And, yes, he should have been glad I had a forgiving nature and everything had turned out okay.

"Babe, I'm so sorry. How are you? How's the baby? Where are you? Are you at the hospital? I'll come. I'll be right there. Just tell me where there is."

"You obviously didn't see all my messages. I'm home. I'm fine. The baby's fine. Just a bit of innocuous spotting caused by its over-horny parents," I explained, letting him off the hook way too easily. But it was Christmastime, and he was stressed by the strike, so I gave him a break.

Jus was just so damn apologetic. You had to hear his tone of voice to fully get what I mean. Then you would recognize the sincerity in it. And the way he was beating himself up. Crap, he did a better job of it than I could do. He was so crazily sorry he had me wanting to comfort him. Apologies weren't just words for Jus. And that's what I loved about him. Part of it, anyway. His genuine concern.

"It's all right, Jus. I saw the news. I heard about the strike. I know you've been dealing with it all day." I hesitated, not sure I wanted to hear the answer to the question I was about to ask. "How bad is it?"

He paused, leading me to believe he was going to sugarcoat it. "Bad," he said at last. "It's going to be touch and go for us long after it ends. And it looks like it's going to be a prolonged work stoppage. The nego-tiating teams have packed up and called a cooling-off period. They don't plan to resume talks until next week at the earliest. The union and the ports are too far apart in their demands right now."

I was watching the dark ripples on the lake and drops of rain splatting as a shower moved through. My Christmas cheer completely melted away. "You won't be home tonight, will you?"

I tried not to sound all judgmental and needy. I knew when I married him that Jus was married to his work as well. And that he felt responsible for the jobs of all his employees. The health of the company meant more than just money for us. It meant livelihoods for thousands of people.

It was just that when I agreed to convince the world I was married to him, I hadn't been in love with him or pregnant with his baby. So I hadn't cared. In fact, I'd been almost relieved. Things were different now.

"I wish I could come home. I'm beat. But there's too much to do. No retailer across the country will be sleeping tonight. This affects us all. We'll be up all night with the workarounds..."

I listened to him vent. He sounded tired and spent. But I knew him. He'd down another can of energy drink and keep going.

"Am I going to see you at all between now and Christmas?" I tried to make my tone light and teasing. But I wasn't sure I'd succeeded.

He snorted. "Maybe. If you come to the office." He inhaled deeply.

"Do you want me to send you your pillow and a blanket?" I joked.

"Are you kicking me out?"

"Are you crazy? No!" I laughed softly, but I was deeply disappointed and worried. "Just trying to make you comfy at your new digs."

"Kay, I'm sorry. This isn't what I'd planned. I know how much you love the holidays—"

"Do what you have to, Jus. Just don't forget about me."

"Never." He paused. "Thanks for understanding. I love you."

I loved him, too. More than I cared to admit. I was going to marry that man. Really marry him. No matter how many obstacles the holiday season threw in my path.

CHAPTER SIX

Kayla

The port strike had made it blatantly clear that I was going to have to marry Jus on Christmas Eve. And not a day sooner. Jus wouldn't break away until he was sure all of Flash's Christmas orders had shipped, the customers were happy, and Flash was out of danger. Challenges, challenges.

I was undeterred. Fate could throw whatever it liked at me. It could be a complete bah humbug. But I was marrying my guy if I had to squeeze the wedding into the season with a red and green shoehorn. Wedge it right in like a foot into a too-tall designer heel.

The more I thought about getting married on Christmas Eve, the more I liked it. It was even better than Valentine's Day! For the rest of our lives we could give each other gifts that were also secret anniversary gifts. Yes, better and better.

It would be our very own tradition. Something we'd started. Something secret to us. Christmas would be our holiday in so many ways.

As I plotted my Christmas wedding, I got a text from my mom: *Does Justin like cinnamon rolls? Should I make my cinnamon roll Christmas tree for Christmas brunch this year?*

I rolled my eyes. Who didn't love cinnamon rolls? But this was Mom's subtle manipulation in her bid to win more time with us over Christmas.

I hesitated. Maybe if I was noncommittal but replied that of course he loved cinnamon rolls, I would be in the clear.

Before I could answer, I got a text from Justin's mom, Diana. *Booking our flight to the Bahamas. We can leave as late as five and still make it to the Bahamas in time to settle in before the tournament begins the next day. What do you think? Justin isn't answering my texts.*

Oh, boy. I made up my mind then and there. I was going to put an end to this war of the Greens and Lucases. And establish a precedent—Jus and I did our own thing for Christmas. At least this year, we did.

We were fighting an unwinnable battle. No matter what we did, one set of parents was going to be miffed. So if they were both miffed together, at least they would be equal. No one could accuse us of playing favorites.

As much as I loved my parents, I loved Jus more. I couldn't tell them what I was really up to. If I could, they would back me completely. And insist on coming along. So they would just have to trust me this year. And understand that I wanted to whisk Jus off for a romantic first Christmas together.

The only problem remaining was Dex. How was I going to convince him to be our witness on Christmas Eve and take a red-eye home for Christmas morning?

If this Christmas Eve wedding was going to happen, I had to meet with our lawyer Harry Lawrence and get him to get that twenty-four-hour waiver.

Harry was Justin's personal lawyer. He also did some work for Flashionista. Harry had drawn up the original legal agreement, the postnuptial agreement, that had guaranteed me ten million dollars for staying with Jus for a year and divorcing on our first anniversary. Jus and I had torn it up when we decided to stay together.

On Wednesday morning, I packed a bag for Jus so he had more than a change of clothes at work if he needed. I also packed his pillow, a spare Christmas blanket, and those Mr. Claus socks. Once he discovered how comfy they were, he would wear them. I knew he would.

I loaded them in the car and headed out for my emergency appointment with Harry.

Harry was the kind of guy who looked like he was born to wear a suit. He had that kind of build. He was classically good looking. So handsome that his looks were wasted in the law profession. He really should have been a model.

Harry and I had started off on the wrong foot when we first met last June and he'd had me served with divorce papers for a marriage I hadn't participated in. At the time, I'd thought someone was pranking me. And that Harry was an arrogant douche.

For his part, Harry had believed I was a gold digger after Justin's money. Since then we'd gotten to know each other and realized that our first impressions had been off. He was still mainly Justin's guy. But he'd helped me out with some of our charitable foundation work, too.

His office suite was decorated for Christmas in tasteful blue and silver. There was a freshly cut tree in the lobby. Innocuous holiday music played softly in the background.

After settling into his office and closing the door, I came right to the point. "I want to marry Jus in New York State on Christmas Eve. I need you to do several things for me to make it happen. First, I need you to draw up a postnuptial prenup giving me the original ten million dollars Jus promised me should we ever divorce. Which we won't.

"I would have you make it for one dollar. But I know Jus wouldn't go for that. The point is I want Jus to know I'm not marrying him for his money. He can't really argue with the sum he originally named. Ten million is nothing to him.

"Second, I need a judicial order waiving the twenty-four-hour waiting period so we can fly into New York for Christmas Eve morning, get the license, and be married immediately.

"Third, the marriage records have to be sealed as private so they aren't published to the public record. Fourth, I need an officiant who requires a second license. Should you handle that or should I get Justin's private investigation firm on it—"

"Wait. Stop. Slow down." Harry leaned back in his desk chair. "Why do you want to get married in New York? As far as any legal or governing authority is concerned, you're already legally married."

I explained my motivation, what I had found out, and how I wanted the marriage to be unassailably genuine and legal.

Harry waited for me to finish, and then broke into his counterargument. Typical for Harry. "While I understand your desire to marry Justin and sign a license yourself, why court trouble?"

I frowned. "What trouble?"

He hesitated. "If the paparazzi gets wind of any of this, they'll have a field day. The more people you involve, the officiant, for example, the greater the chance the truth gets out. Why risk it?"

I shook my head gently, disappointed in him. But not surprised by his caution. "You're clearly not a romantic, Harry. Which is just too bad. You could be some girl's knight triumphant." I smiled to soften my statement. I was only half teasing.

"Love is worth taking any chance for. I want to be genuinely married to Jus. I want to vow to love him for my entire lifetime. And you, of all people, should be able to see that a legitimate marriage would silence all critics and any legal challenges."

The baby chose that moment to kick me. Hard. It took my breath away. I winced and rubbed my belly to soothe her, which drew Harry's gaze to my baby bump.

"Prenup. Postnup. Or whatever the hell it would be now. Even as your lawyer, I'm losing track. I'll draw something up if you insist. But if I know Justin, he won't sign it, no matter what the dollar amount." Harry frowned in thought. "I'm not sure about the legality of a postnup prenup. There's no case law that I know of. How the hell would it stand up in court?"

He shook his head. "You don't need one, anyway. That baby is your insurance. Justin will take care of that baby no matter what."

"I want postnup prenup, anyway. It may be an empty gesture, but it's the thought that counts. Isn't that what they say?" I held his gaze.

Harry nodded and slapped his desk. "If that's what you want. Our office has a branch in New York. We should be able to handle everything. I'll get on this right away."

I smiled at him, relieved.

After I left Harry's office, I made my weekly Wednesday visit to the children's hospital. Jus used to go on his own. Then I joined him. And since peak had hit, I'd mostly been going on my own. Jus gave huge sums to the hospital. It was easy to see why. The children and their illnesses and triumphs would win over the hardest heart.

I was on a mission to make sure every child that was in the hospital on Christmas or Christmas Eve got a special present. With that in mind, I was keeping an eye on the long-term patients, those I knew had little chance of being discharged for Christmas. I'd been subtly questioning them and helping them write their letters to Santa.

On my way from the hospital to Flashionista, I stopped by the bakery up the hill from Flash and bought out their selection of holiday cookies to take to the office. And a nice stuffed meat pastry for Jus for lunch. I had a meeting with Britt, Sarah, and Marla, the head merch buyer, to discuss the upcoming Santa Sample Sale.

I showed up at Flash carrying a box of snowflake cookies, Justin's pillow and lunch, and wheeling his suitcase.

Justin

My phone rang as I was coming out of our latest meeting. *Mom.* She knew better than to call me at work. She'd been texting all morning. I hadn't had time to answer.

I picked up as I walked into my office and closed the door. "Mother."

She hated being called mother. I used the term in a jokey, reprimanding way. In that tone of voice she liked to use on me when I was in trouble.

"Justin Arnold Green," she responded just as quickly in the same mock reprimand.

We broke out laughing together.

"You're finally taking your old mother's calls now, are you?"

"Only because if I don't, you'll call out the National Guard."

"Oh, I don't think I'm happy enough with you to do that. I'd rather keep texting and calling until I drive you crazy."

She was still teasing. Sort of. There was a biting edge to her sense of humor.

"I've been swamped all day. A little thing called a port closure has had my attention."

"Yes, I know. I do watch the news from time to time." Her tone softened. "And it's peak. We're all busy. Dad and I are scrambling to get the last-minute travel arrangements made for the teams and put the rugby tournament schedule together."

"I didn't raise a wimp or a quitter. You'll handle it. You always do."

I appreciated her vote of confidence, but I hadn't dealt with a shipping stoppage of this magnitude before. And certainly never during peak.

"I'm sure you don't have much time, so I'll keep this brief," she said. "I need to know your plans for Christmas so I can finalize our travel plans. You'll be here on Christmas Eve after dinner and on Christmas morning, right? Isn't that our allotted time slot?"

It was more a directive than a question. Mom was used to coaching and commanding. She didn't take a backseat to anyone, least of all me. The fact that I was a billionaire didn't impress her much. It would have been better if I'd been a professional athlete.

"I'm glad you called about that," I said, trying to catch her off guard. "I've been meaning to talk to you about Christmas. I may be able to arrange to spend Christmas morning with you, if you'll do something for me."

"Justin." The frown in her voice was deep. "Some things never change. You've been negotiating since you were little." She gave a heavy sigh. "What am I going to have to trade to get a little time with my baby boy on Christmas?"

"For one thing, you can stop calling me your baby boy."

She laughed. "And for another?"

I hesitated. My mom wasn't a girly girl in any sense of the word. She was a complete extroverted tomboy, a girl jock. Which was part of the reason she and I had never understood each other. I was the black sheep of my family—the introverted non-athlete of her trio of boys. The only introvert in the family. She and Dad were both as extroverted as they came. Which explained why they loved team sports so much. If I had been athletic, I would have done an individual sport like track or tennis. Team bonding didn't appeal to me.

Mom was impossible to buy for. She didn't like jewelry, which I could get awesome deals on. Or trendy fashions. And perfume and anything scented gave her a headache. Basically, anything Flashionista carried, except maybe for a few odd housewares, were not my mom's thing.

She also wasn't the type of woman who enjoyed the arts. Give her a rugby, hockey, or football game any day of the week. Just don't make her watch the ballet. I was about to call her bluff. The secret to negotiating was to have something the other person either desperately needed or wanted. I had the upper hand.

"I'll give you your Christmas morning for the pleasure of your company at *The Nutcracker* on Christmas Eve. With the caveat that you have to convince Dad, Jerod, and Jeremy to come, too."

"You bought tickets to a Christmas ballet for *our* family? Have you lost your mind?" She laughed.

"Not just ours. Kayla's, too. I went to a lot of trouble to get tickets for *both* families. So Kay and I could spend Christmas Eve with *all* the people we love."

"Oh, bleh. Don't make me gag," she said. "You're really laying it on thick, boy-o." There was a shudder in Mom's voice. "Did those Lucases put you up to this?"

"No. *Kay* loves *The Nutcracker.* It's a surprise for her." I was taking pleasure in Mom's discomfort. "It's on me. And dinner after. At Dad's favorite steakhouse on the waterfront to make it up to you and the brothers." I grinned. "You can get all dressed up. Behave yourself and I'll buy you a new evening gown."

Another point for me. I couldn't remember the last time I'd seen my mom in a dress of any kind. She belonged to the pantsuit set.

"How did I raise such an evil boy?" But she laughed.

Mom's favorite attire was a tracksuit or sweats. When she had to dress up, she wore slacks. I was pushing her hard.

"Make it a pantsuit and I'm in."

Did I call it or what?

"A dressy pantsuit," I said. "With some sparkle to it. And heels. Nothing less than two inches."

"You're pushing your luck," she said.

"Deal?" I had her on the ropes.

"Deal." She paused and broke into her evil winner's cackle. "Sucker! How many times have I told you to do your research, Justin? I've actually been wanting to see this new *Nutcracker*. See if it lives up to its predecessor.

"The last time I went was before you were born. With my grandma the year before she died. Fond memories. Fond memories. Your dad has refused to take me again all these years. He'll have to cave now, won't he?"

"How do you know I didn't do my research, Ma?" I paused for emphasis. But, of course, I hadn't. "How do you know I'm not just trying to please you, too?"

"Nice try!"

I pictured Mom shaking her head.

"One more thing. This is a surprise for Kay. I haven't told her about it yet. Just make sure she doesn't hear about it until she hears it from me."

Kayla

I knocked on Justin's office door and poked my head in without waiting for his reply. "Jus?"

He was just finishing up a call. Was it my imagination, or did he pale and look like I'd caught him in the middle of some clandestine act? I looked around the room, suspiciously, then back to him.

He recovered quickly. "Kay!" His face lit up.

He set the phone down and jumped up to greet me as I struggled to wheel his suitcase in and balanced the box of cookies and his lunch, with his pillow pressed beneath my arm.

I managed to get in the door by the time he reached me.

He took in the suitcase and pillow and frowned as he took the box of cookies from me. "Are you sure you're not throwing me out?" His eyes sparkled like he was teasing. But there was just enough doubt in his voice to be completely sweet and adorable.

Jus still didn't realize how hot and attractive he was. Which made him even hotter.

"And softening the blow with a box of sugar cookies?" I laughed. "Should I be? Throwing you out? I already promised I wouldn't."

I tossed the pillow on his sofa, let go of his suitcase, and threw my arms around him, almost knocking him over with my passion and the element of surprise. The cookie box tipped precariously. He recovered just in time to save it.

I pulled him into an embrace while he balanced the cookies with one hand and caressed my belly with the other. I always missed him. Being in his arms now reminded me just how much I loved him.

"How's my baby?" he said to my bump.

I tipped his chin up. "I thought *I* was your baby."

"It's an all-encompassing term these days." He set the cookies down, put his hands on either side of my baby bump, jostling it while he distracted me again with a deep, sensual kiss.

"Hey!" I said, pulling away. "I know this trick. You're trying to wake her up so you can feel her kick."

"I miss her." He grinned and squeezed me tight to make a point. And get the response he wanted. The baby kicked. Hard.

Jus grinned. "I felt that! There's my girl."

"I think your girl is going to be a rugby player. Which will make your mom happy. Baby girl kicks like your brothers."

Jus shrugged and kissed me again. "It runs in the family."

I smacked my lips and looked upward, trying to place the taste of him. "Your kiss on my lips tastes like an energy drink." I pulled away to study him. "Have you had anything else to eat or drink since you left home?"

He made an exaggerated point of thinking my question over, like it was rocket science or something. "That would be no. Don't need it. One case of energy drinks a day and I'm golden."

I grabbed his arm. "Hold your hand out."

"Looking for a tremble, are you, my suspicious babe?" He held his hand out. It was steadier than mine.

"That's scary," I said. "You've built up an inhuman tolerance for sugar and caffeine."

He laughed again.

"I miss you," I said, as my heart squeezed with want. "Promise me you'll come home at least *once* before Christmas. Otherwise, I'll feel neglected. And I might have to take a lover."

His gaze fell to my bump and he raised one eyebrow.

I laughed. "Some guys find this hot."

"You mean me?" His grin was adorable. He leaned in and whispered in my ear. "I'll be home soon. My need for sex is about to overwhelm my sense of duty. I wish I didn't have a meeting to go to in a few minutes."

"That's all I am to you, now, is it?" I teased. "A roly-poly sex object?"

"And a baby machine. Don't forget that part. A billionaire like me needs an heir."

I punched him playfully.

He looked at the pillow and suitcase. "So what *is* this?"

"Making you comfortable. I figured you'd want an extra change of clothes." I held up the bag with his meaty pastry. "And this is lunch. Or dinner. For whenever you finally remember to eat. Put it in your fridge."

I hugged him, making a point of feeling him up. "You're getting too skinny," I said, imitating Mrs. Claus.

"So, did I interrupt something important?" I kissed him lightly again. "You look guilty."

"You're mistaking surprise and happiness for guilt. Did you really come all the way downtown to bring me my pillow?"

"And lunch. Don't forget lunch." I kissed him lightly again and let him go, reluctantly. "Actually, I have a meeting with the merch buyers in a few minutes to discuss the sample sale. You're not the only one with a busy schedule."

"So *you* squeezed *me* in." His look was penetrating and sexy.

"Yeah. I guess I did."

"And you brought me a whole box of cookies? Are these supposed to last the entire season?"

I shook my head. "Hands off! Those are for the merch department. There's one for you in the bag with your lunch."

His admin poked her head in his office. "Justin? There's a representative from the port here to meet with you."

"That's okay," I said to Jus. "I have to run anyway or I'll be late, too."

I kissed him once more and we were both off to our respective meetings. Walking through the building, I thought how fun it would be eventually to work here, too. The charity work and the pregnancy were keeping me busy. For now. But I had big ideas for Flash, too.

The Flashionista offices were a dream come true to anyone who loved retail, photography, or fashion. They shot their daily online catalogue onsite. And even though they had already blown past Christmas and were shooting January spots, Christmas props were still strewn everywhere. There were racks and racks of clothes, neatly organized for the fashion shoots, makeup artists, hair stylists, artist, models, and flashing lights.

Every desk in the merch department was decorated for the owner's holiday of choice—Christmas, Kwanza, Hanukkah, or just plain winter. There was clearly a competition going on. The transportation, legal, and supplier management departments were definitely losing, as far as decorating went.

I grabbed the holiday wish box on my way in to the conference room. Britt and Sarah were already waiting for me.

"Look at you, baby mama!" Britt jumped to her feet to hug me.

Sarah squealed, too.

They'd been sitting at a conference table, drinking coffee. Britt hugged me so enthusiastically, I almost lost my cookies. The holiday cookies I was holding. Those cookies had a death wish. Suicide by tumbling and crumbling seemed to be their main agenda.

"Can I feel it? Can I feel it? Can I feel it?" Britt put her hands on my baby bump, mimicking the people who came up to me thinking they had a right to a feel.

There was something about a pregnant belly that made people ignore personal space and social niceties and boundaries. And feel that your body was public property.

I rolled my eyes and laughed. She knew how much I hated it when complete strangers came up and put their hands on my body like we were intimates.

"She's not moving." Britt bounced my belly. "And a little round belly that shook when she laughed like a bowl full of—"

The baby stretched and moved. I winced. "Now you did it! You woke her up." But I said it jovially. "You and Jus, you're terrible."

I grabbed Britt's hand and put it on the spot a tiny baby foot was moving across my stomach.

Sarah took the cookies and wish box from me and set them on the table.

"FYI, this is way better than a bowl full of jelly," Britt said.

She finally let me go so I could hug Sarah.

"Where's Marla?" I asked, looking around for the head of the merchandise department.

"She's in another meeting," Britt said. "One of the thousands regarding the port strike. She'll be late. She said to start without her."

We all took a seat. Britt grabbed a cookie while I opened the wish box. It was packed.

"Oh boy," I said as I opened it and began handing them out for us to sort and catalogue. "Maybe we should have made this digital."

"We still can from here on out," Britt said.

Sarah put her mouth to one side. "Wow! The requests have suddenly started pouring in since Thanksgiving. We pretty much had all the items people wanted up through the last time we looked before break. Getting all this"—she pointed to the pile of requests—"is going to be a problem. And a time suck. Since this port closure, everyone is trying to keep their head above water dealing with our suppliers."

Britt frowned. "And it's still three weeks until Christmas."

"We'll think of something," I said. "I'll talk to Jus about hiring a temp to sort through everything and match the samples with the wishes."

"That would be awesome!" Sarah said.

We dug in and began reading through the pile of wants. We had just finished cataloguing the employee wants and were discussing what items would be left to give to the families at the hospital with Marla walked in. She looked harried and tired.

"Sorry I'm late." She took a seat and grabbed a cookie. "What did I miss?"

"We were just about to discuss how we're going to deliver the presents to the children's hospital," I said. "I was thinking we'd hire a delivery service to truck them over. And someone to play Santa Claus and hand them out on Christmas Eve afternoon. The kids will like that."

Marla shook her head. "No. That won't work. Justin *always* delivers the presents after the employee party on Christmas Eve. He loves it. He wouldn't miss it for the world. It's tradition. The children expect him. And it's fabulous PR for Flash. The media eats it up. He reads the kids 'The Night Before Christmas' and brings them cookies and milk." She turned to me. "I'm surprised he hasn't mentioned it to you."

CHAPTER SEVEN

Kayla

Of course he delivered the presents! Why was I not surprised by this latest roadblock? Once again my special gift to Jus was going to make me look like a great big Christmas-spirit-killing bitch.

And as for tradition—how traditional could Jus handing out the presents be? Flashionista was only, like, four years old to begin with. I mean, Jus had just turned twenty-two last summer. It wasn't like there had been a lot of time to establish timeworn traditions.

Marla's adamant attitude irritated me, too. It was so superior and knowing.

Because it was the Christmas season, it was my duty to spread good cheer. Which meant I had to be the bigger person.

"No, I didn't know! But that's just like Jus." I beamed, genuinely proud of him and his generous spirit. "He's *always* thinking of others. And working hard. Especially with this port strike."

I leaned toward Marla, making her my confidante. "This is just between those of us here. I've already planned something special for Jus on Christmas Eve. I'm sorry I didn't know about Jus delivering gifts to the children at the hospital. I really am.

"But my plans are made now. And can't be undone. If I'd known earlier about the children's hospital...

"But that's beside the point now. I hope you'll help me out." He and me and baby-to-be were a family. And soon we'd be a real, legal family.

I was beginning to feel a lot like the Velveteen Rabbit, wanting to be a real wife. Wasn't that a Christmas story, too? My mom used to read it to me at Christmas when I was little.

Marla lifted an eyebrow, but she looked suddenly sentimental and apologetic. "Yes, how could you know?" she said more kindly. "He's been so consumed with running things, it probably slipped his mind."

I nodded. "He's barely even been home since Thanksgiving. How about Riggins?" I said, trying to find a solution. "Riggins is totally charming. Everyone loves him. He might like a turn—"

Marla laughed. "You obviously don't know Riggins well enough. The hospital has always been Justin's thing. I think children actually scare Riggins."

"He doesn't like them?" I was surprised.

Marla shrugged. "He's not comfortable around them. Let's leave it at that."

Sarah and Britt had gone surprisingly quiet while they watched the show between Marla and me. I almost asked them if they'd like popcorn with their show. Britt had only hired on to Flash last summer and Sarah had only been with Flash slightly longer. Neither had a dog in this fight.

"I love the children at the hospital, too." I took a deep breath. "We all want the best for them and their families. We still have time. We'll work *something* out. I still think hiring a topnotch Santa might be the thing."

After my meeting, I stopped by Justin's office to say goodbye. He was deep in concentration, doing something on his computer.

"I'm heading out," I said.

"Do I get a goodbye kiss?" He came to me and pulled me into his arms.

"Jus?" I bit my lip. "About Christmas—"

"Yes?"

"What do you want for Christmas this year?" It had occurred to me that I really hadn't asked him. I wasn't really having second thoughts or backing down. But I didn't want to ram my will through and deprive him of something that gave him joy. Like delivering presents to the children. If there was something Jus wanted more...

"You." His answer was quick and his grin positively lecherous.

"I'm serious." I sighed. "This is our first year together. I want it to be special."

"So do I." He got that look on his face that made me think he was up to something.

Oh, crap. He probably had a beautiful surprise gift for me and was going to give it to me in some romantic way.

"So if we change up the way things have been done in the past, that would be okay with you?" Maybe I wasn't exactly fighting fair here. But I was desperate.

His face lit up. "What do you mean?"

"Like start new traditions," I said. "Our own traditions."

"Absolutely! I'm all for new traditions. Especially if they make you happy."

He was so enthusiastic. I didn't want to spoil it by going into details just now. "You haven't answered my question."

He thought for a minute while I stared at him, wondering how I'd been so lucky to be thrown into a fake marriage with him.

He cupped my face gently. "I want something only you can give me. Your love. Your loyalty. Your friendship."

My heart beat with joy. I was on the right track. I was going to give him exactly what he wanted.

"I give that to you every day," I said. "I love you."

"And I never take it for granted. Just keep on loving me, and I'm good."

Friday, December 5th

Kayla

By Friday, I was in a state of sublime happiness. I had convinced Jus we needed to hire a temp to deal with the flood of Christmas wishes coming in. I'd decided on a small town on the Hudson River outside of New York City to get married in. It was perfect. On the Hudson River. Quaint and scenic. A small international airport was nearby.

There was no point trying to fly into New York City on one of the busiest travel days of the year and get to the Office of the City Clerk of New York through traffic. That was madness.

Harry called. He'd found a clergyman from the little town to marry us. One who waved all premarital counseling. Since we were married already, it only made sense. His name was Pastor James Brown. He believed in love enough to perform a ceremony on Christmas Eve, and yet required that essential second license.

I liked him already. He had a certain amount of essential cynicism. For a nominal fee, he would perform the ceremony at the quaint, picturesque wedding chapel I'd found, and booked, on the river. I had it for the entire day. Not that I needed if for more than about an hour, if that.

It looked lovely in the pictures. I hoped it lived up to its online hype as a beautiful venue for intimate winter weddings. However it turned out, it couldn't be any tackier than where Jus had supposedly married me in the first place.

I didn't want a reputation for getting married in blatantly tasteless settings time and again. However, beggars couldn't be choosers, especially at this late date. With all the Christmas travellers and celebrations, I was lucky to find any venue available at all. Then again, I'd been willing to pay a premium price.

I'd found a florist and ordered a bouquet and two boutonnieres to be delivered to the chapel. Jus was colorblind and couldn't see most shades of pink. But he was good with deep red. The red and white Christmas roses I ordered would be perfect.

I was having a cake flown in from a top bakery in New York City. Christmas themed. Single tier. White cake with raspberry filling. Justin's favorite. White fondant icing with delicate, intricate scrollwork, and red gum-paste roses and poinsettias crafted by an artist to look positively real. Also delivered to the chapel. Along with a bottle of the best champagne available. For a bridal toast.

Ordering a cake was probably over the top. We weren't having a reception. But I dreamed of cutting the cake with my groom and feeding Jus that first bite.

When I checked in with Harry, he said we should have our waiver by the end of next week. Jus had a tux that would be perfect to be married in. Now I just needed a dress and shoes...

All these lovely winter wedding thoughts were still bouncing through my mind like happy wishes for Santa when Jus and I boarded Riggins' yacht for the Christmas Ship Parade that evening.

We made our way to the lower deck. Jus tucked me in his arms. We were soon parading around Lake Washington in the middle of a Christmas ship flotilla.

When had "parading around" become an insult? As in "stop parading around!" Which had been a favorite of my mom when I was little.

This parading was merry and jolly, totally in the spirit of the season. Riggins had equipped his yacht with a powerful, clear sound system and mics, and a top-of-the-line karaoke system. He and Jus and a couple of the other guys from Flash loved to sing. Once a month, they sang karaoke at a local pub during the Flash employees' happy hour.

Riggins had also amply stocked the booze for this cruise. After the stress of the past week, everyone needed to let off steam and relax. And speaking of steam, every guest had a steaming hot cocktail of their choice—a hot buttered rum, a hot toddy, maybe an Irish coffee, or a Tom and Jerry.

I loved Tom and Jerrys. They reminded me of my grandpa. But Riggins talked me into an English Bishop, a traditional British hot cocktail made with port, orange, and cloves. Riggins was half British. He insisted I try it, saying it was Scrooge's favorite drink. The reformed Scrooge who woke after the last spirit left.

I was off hard alcohol for the duration. But a few sips of wine were fine.

The lead ship in this parade was a local dinner cruise ship equipped with a sound system and a professional choir who belted out traditional, choir-ish music at every stop and in between. The music was beautiful. And a little sedate if you were in the partying mood.

The boats in the flotilla spanned the range from just a step up from rowboat to the large cruise ship, but from smallest to largest, they were all elaborately decorated.

Riggins had spared no expense for his decorations. Every line of his yacht was trimmed with lights programmed to put on a light show timed to music. As the choir sang, they were rather serenely humming along in patient slow motion. A large wireframe tree with a sparkling star on top was in the middle of the lower deck.

The night was clear. The moon was out. And despite the wakes from the other boats, the lake was nearly as smooth as glass. Dark and bottomless and reflecting the moon in silver shimmers.

Sound carried so well at night across the water, we almost didn't need our speakers. The carols swept across to the shores as we cruised past Coulon Park packed with people waiting to see the ship parade. Past the Clam Lights put on by Ivar's, a fabulous lights display complete with tall wireframe running clams with legs. Past lakefront houses where homeowners gathered on their lawns and docks with mugs of steaming beverages and waved and caroled back to us.

In December in Seattle, you couldn't depend on nice weather. Certainly not on clear weather. But tonight was perfect. Forty-five degrees and calm. Peace on earth, at least weather-wise.

If you haven't experienced Christmas caroling like this, it's hard to understand the fun and sense of kindred spirit with the other boats and the people onshore. Everyone was in a merry mood, laughing and shouting between boats. Waving. Singing.

I was warm and toasty in my red Christmas sweater with the faux-fur collar and matching hat and gloves, wrapped in Justin's arms. And, of course, I had the little baby heat engine inside me to warm me up from the inside out.

I was so incredibly happy Justin had taken the night off. After the port closed, I'd been worried Riggins would cancel the outing. Now I was grateful for him for insisting that the party must go on. The entire top brass of Flash was out on the boat. So who was manning the store? Brave of them to all abandon store for ship.

Jus snuggled into me from behind, singing commandingly and beautifully. I lost myself in his deep, sexy, beautiful voice. He had a way of infusing the music with passion that swept me away.

Next to us, Riggins flashed Jus a look of exasperation as the choir broke into yet *another* slow carol. Clearly, he wanted to party.

Jus leaned down and whispered, "I don't hear you singing."

"You know I don't sing. I hope the baby gets your talent." I took a sip of my Bishop and leaned my head back against his chest.

"You sang to me once."

I smiled up at him. "Only because it was a desperate situation."

We motored around the lake in dark mode, following the lead ship, lights off except for Christmas lights. When our Christmas ship parade tour of the lake was

over, Riggins pulled up in front of his lakefront mansion and dropped anchor offshore away from the dock.

He turned to Jus. "Let's give my neighbors a show,
people."

"Who are we serenading?" one of the guys said.
"There's no one out here, Riggins."

Riggins shook his head. "If we sing, they will come. I
promised them we'd carol for them again this year. I
don't go back on my word." He laughed. "'Jingle Bells,'
everyone. Jack, hit the speakers and the music."

He handed Jus a mic. "Justin and I will lead. On
three! One, two, three!"

We broke into a rowdy, jazzy version, accompanied
by the karaoke music in the background.

Riggins kept singing and turning up the volume until one by one neighbor after neighbor appeared until
he had a crowd. They applauded and raised their glasses to us from shore. Jus and Riggins were high on the
thrill of performing, and hammed it up.

"Okay, that's it, people. Show's over!" Riggins finally said. "Merry Christmas! Happy holidays! Thanks for
coming. We appreciate your support!" He saluted the
crowd. "Hit the lights! Let's get this party started."

The appetizers and booze started flowing. Riggins
fired up the karaoke. The sounds of a jazzy Christmas
filled the air.

Riggins had hired a caterer and a bartender. And a
professional captain to pilot the boat. Leaving Riggins
free to imbibe Christmas cocktails to his heart's content, both warm and chilled.

I angled to get him alone so I could speak to him while he was in a warm, happy holiday mood.

Justin's friend and mentor, Lazer Grayson, came over to congratulate him. "That was an even better performance by you and Riggins than last year."

"Yeah. We've been practicing. Long hours at the office," Jus said. "We had to do something to combat fatigue."

"Singing invigorates you, obviously," Lazer said.

"That and half a dozen energy drinks kept me going forty-eight hours straight," Jus said.

I shuddered at the thought.

"How are things going with the port? Any word on when the strike will end..."

This could be a long conversation, I thought.

I tapped Jus on the arm and motioned that I was going to the head. A convenient excuse. With the baby jumping on my bladder, I was constantly going to the little girls' room.

I slipped away and cornered Riggins. Christmas music was blasting, making confidential conversation impossible. I grabbed his arm and shouted in his ear, "Can I have a word? In private."

He took my arm. "This way."

As he led me up the stairs to the upper deck, he shouted and pointed above our heads. A ball of mistletoe hung above us. "I hope no one gets the wrong idea."

"Justin's not the jealous type." I kissed Riggins lightly on the cheek. "Merry Christmas, Riggins."

He laughed.

Riggins had the looks, charm, and charisma that made women notice him everywhere he went.

"Everyone gets the wrong idea all the time," I said without a hint of flirt in my voice. "It goes with the territory of being in the spotlight." I rubbed my baby bump. "This pretty much guarantees people won't talk. Who would sneak away with an obviously pregnant woman?"

Riggins smiled. "You're still beautiful, Kayla."

"That's sweet of you to say. And prudent. If you'd told me I'm glowing, I'd have had to cause a scene," I said. "This time of year, glowing is only for reindeers' noses."

"And drunks," Riggins said. "So what's up?"

I looked around to make sure no one would overhear, and leaned in and whispered to him, "Justin needs Christmas Eve off. All of Christmas Eve. Not just a half-day. And all of the night of the 23rd."

"Oh?" Riggins looked intrigued. "I'm not his boss. We're partners. I don't have any say—"

"I think you do," I said, flattering him. "You have plenty of influence over him. If you suggest it, encourage him to take the time off, and cover for him, he'll fall happily into my evil plan to whisk him away for a few days."

Riggins laughed. "Evil plan? On December 23rd? Daredevil. You're not worried about being on Santa's naughty list?"

"Mark my words, I *plan* to be on his naughty list." I winked at Riggins.

His eyes sparkled, reflecting the Christmas lights around us. "Lucky Justin."

"I want my husband back for at least a few days during the holidays." At the thought of my wedding, happiness bubbled up. I didn't see any reason to hide my joy. "I've planned a special surprise getaway for him and me. I need your help pulling it off."

"A surprise?" Riggins got a funny look on his face. "I'm not a fan of surprises. They backfire too often."

"Now who's being a killjoy?" I teased. "I thought you had more adventure in you." I paused. "I'm not asking much from you. Just keep it a secret. And I would really appreciate it if you'd take over the gift-giving duties at the hospital Christmas Eve. And running the company party the morning of the 24th."

I grabbed Riggins' arm and implored him with my pitiful, frail pregnant woman look. "This is our first Christmas together. I really want to make it special before Jus and I become parents."

I batted my eyes at Riggins shamelessly and exaggeratedly. "This would mean a lot to me," I said in a singsong tone. "I'd owe you big time. What if I promise Jus will take New Year's Eve duty. If he can have Christmas Eve—"

Riggins stared at me.

I was losing him. "What?" I said. "What's wrong?"

"I have a condition." He seemed almost amused.

I dropped his arm and put my on my negotiating face. "Name it."

"I'll do everything you ask, but—"

"Damn! I hate buts," I said. "They're always harbingers of doom."

"But," Riggins continued, "you have to tell him about this 'surprise' as soon as possible."

"That's an impossible condition." I put my hands on my nearly nonexistent hips to let him know I meant business. They'd melded with my waist and my baby bump. "If I tell him, it won't be a surprise, then, will it, wise guy."

Riggins shrugged. "Sorry. It's a deal breaker for me if you don't." He turned like he was done and ready to go back to the lower deck.

I caught his arm again. "Wait!"

He paused.

"What do you know? Why is it so important that I tell Jus?"

"So he can be prepared. I told you, I don't like surprises. I refuse to be part of one. Especially at Christmas." He smiled at me. "Believe me. Justin will be much happier knowing about your plans in advance."

Riggins was a fierce negotiator. I read people pretty well. I could tell he wasn't going to budge on this one.

"All right," I said, and stuck out my hand. "Deal."

He grinned that grin people get when they've pulled one over on you and shook my hand. "Deal. The sooner you tell him, the better. If he doesn't know by"—he glanced at a calendar on his phone—"December 15th, the deal's off."

"Fine." I shrugged like I didn't care and that I hadn't just had my negotiating head handed to me on a Christmas platter. "I have half a mind to cancel the

Santa I've already hired to help you at the children's hospital."

His answering laugh was as hearty and rich as the Ghost of Christmas Present.

There was a gap between songs. Suddenly, Jus was crooning "Winter Wonderland."

"That's my cue," I said to Riggins. "He's singing my song. I'd better join him." I pointed my finger at Riggins. "Don't you say a word to him until I tell him about the surprise."

I came down the steps from the upper deck just as Jus looked up. Then—yes, I could be a ham—I danced across the deck into his arms and swayed with him to the music as he looked deep into my eyes and sang to me.

Crazily, the clergyman Harry had found was named Brown. I wondered if he would he let us call him parson?

Justin

Riggins pulled me aside as we got off the yacht. "Have you given those *Nutcracker Ballet* tickets to Kayla yet?"

I frowned. "No. Not yet. Why?"

"A word to the wise—do it soon, will you?"

"Why?" I frowned.

"Soon. Trust me." He winked and walked off humming "Joy to the World."

CHAPTER EIGHT

Friday, December 12th

Kayla

Planning a clandestine wedding was not the easiest task to begin with. Not when you were married to, and marrying, a billionaire, a minor celebrity of sorts whose every move was of interest to both the local and national media. Which was why I had booked the wedding chapel under my maiden name, Lucas. Fortunately, a common enough last name to avoid suspicion or a connection to Jus. And my first initial only. And paid the deposit using my old single-girl bank account. Same with the florist.

Harry had sworn Pastor Brown to secrecy, in the form of a legal nondisclosure agreement. Standard operating procedure? Definitely not. But what was standard about our marriage? The uniqueness of it was part of the beauty of it, right? Our wedding and marriage were as inimitable as our love. That sounded romantic, didn't it?

Our wedding records would not be published as part of the public record. Even so, I was getting twitchy with worry that somehow news would slip out. *Thanks a lot for that, Harry.* The thing was, I didn't need a fancy wedding so much as I just wanted to get married. Was that so much to ask? Apparently, it was.

I would have married Jus at the airport, if that had been at all feasible.

At one point, I even panicked, and looked up whether an airline captain could marry us. So what if we just flew over New York airspace, got married, and flew right back to Seattle? Would that count as legal?

Unfortunately, the main answer I found seemed to be "no." Airline pilots could not. Not unless they were also a licensed celebrant of New York. Ha! I liked that word, used on many wedding websites, *way* better than officiant. Much happier and joyful. And even then, I wondered if just being in New York airspace would be enough.

The last thing I wanted, or needed, was another questionably legal marriage. And just try to find a private business jet pilot licensed to perform marriages in New York and who required a second license before he or she would perform the ceremony. If that didn't raise a few eyebrows, what would? And, who, exactly, would be flying the plane during the ceremony? Would the pilot conduct it from the cockpit?

Plus there was still the little matter of applying for the license. We couldn't do that from the air. Too bad. Online wedding applications, the wave of the future?

Add to all this planning a wedding on top of all the Christmas parties I was responsible for. But I finally had those under control. Delegate. That was the key. Let go of any, and all, control-freak tendencies. Let the professionals handle it. Crap, I was becoming a pampered princess.

I'd handed the children's hospital party off to a professional party planner along with a fat check and instructions to hire a genuinely kind, highly authentic Santa with a real white beard. Riggins would thank me.

Justin's assistant Danielle had been swamped since the port closure. So now, thanks to me, the party for the employees was also in the competent hands of the same professional planner. Who'd come highly recommended, and was insanely busy and in demand. But money really does talk. And gobs of money practically screams. Which was so nice when you really need it to.

With Magda's help—she'd helped Jus with the parties before I'd come on the scene—the party at our home for the upper management team was well in hand. The caterers were hired. The menu planned. The decorating done. The invitations out.

And so were the myriad of holiday cards, which my assistant Andrea and I had spent the better part of two days doing.

Now, with advent half over, my charm bracelet was laden with charms. The seemingly odd and random selection of beads Jus was giving me had puzzled me at first. But with enough beads now, a theme was emerging. Snowflakes, rosebuds, flowers, a fairy, a toy soldier, a glass bead from Spain, a color-changing alexandrite bead from Russia, a queen's crown, a mouse, and a flute. Unless I missed my guess, he would give me a nutcracker bead on Christmas Eve.

I got tears thinking about him sweetly planning this advent bracelet while being crazy busy with peak. Jus was like that, always spoiling me. I didn't really deserve him.

I loved *The Nutcracker* and the music that accompanied it. The story was so romantic. A nutcracker becoming a prince. Fairies and candy and magic!

When I was little, my parents played the music for me while I danced around in my nightgown pretending to be Clara. I played the DVD of the ballet at least half a dozen times each Christmas season.

I took ballet lessons through elementary school. At one point I'd dreamed of joining the Pacific Northwest Ballet and getting the lead part. Sadly, I was neither good enough nor dedicated enough. Then junior high hit and other things had occupied my mind. Like boys.

I wondered how Jus knew. He must have asked Britt.

Jus was such a romantic! For a guy who'd never dated anyone but me, and not even really me when you got down to it, he was so sweetly thoughtful. It was a skill I wanted to learn. Hard as I tried, I never seemed to find a way to outdo him. Not that it was a competition. But I wanted him to know that I loved him as much as he loved me. I was willing to spend a lifetime showing him.

I wanted to spoil him as much as he spoiled me. He had the upper hand—way more resources. I vowed to use what I had to give him all those intangible things. Things money couldn't buy.

When you were wealthy, it was never a given that people were truly your friends. Or that your spouse genuinely loved you. What if they were just pretending to get to your money and influence?

I was going to give Jus love, trust, security, loyalty, and friendship until my dying breath. I wanted him to know that I was the one person in this world that would love him if he were broke.

Riggins' awful threats to back out of covering for Jus on Christmas Eve if I didn't spring my surprise on Jus before this coming Monday, December 15th, had gotten me thinking. Since I couldn't surprise Jus the way I'd originally planned, I would have to do something else romantic. And then the obvious had occurred to me—I would *ask* Jus to marry me. Yes, issue a real marriage proposal. While we were out on a special Christmas season date.

Time was ticking. Each new advent bead Jus gave me for my bracelet marked another day down. The pressure of being as romantic as Jus was mounting. And Jus was so busy, I was having a hard time getting any time with him at all.

So...when Jus suddenly announced he was taking Saturday off to take me downtown to see the annual gingerbread house display that supported juvenile diabetes research, I realized I was going to have to seize my chance. Jus went every year and quietly made a generous donation. Jus loved children, and, having been bullied himself when he was growing up, was especially sympathetic to children who had special needs or circumstances.

Actually, this was perfect! I went every year, too. Usually with Britt and our group of friends. We were always in awe of the elaborate concoctions sponsored by local architecture and designers and made by local master bakers and pastry chefs from the top restaurants around the area. Seeing the displays brought back the holiday excitement of being a girl again.

Time alone with Jus was precious this holiday season, a gift in itself. I was going to make it something we'd always remember.

Every year the gingerbread display had a different theme. I looked this year's theme up—classic Christmas music. Each gingerbread "house" had to represent a popular Christmas song or piece of music. And what do you know? One of the groups had done "Winter Wonderland"!

Perfect. It couldn't have played into my hands better if I had planned it. I would propose, quietly, a mere whisper in his ear, at the gingerbread display! Maybe not even a whisper. Maybe I should give him a card?

The pressure to make a beautiful, romantic proposal was astounding. How did guys do it? How did they handle it? Plus keeping it a secret? I was already about to burst.

The thought of a public proposal was thrilling, adventurous, and daring. There wasn't much chance of me getting down on one knee. In my current preggo state, I would be lucky to get back up again. My center of gravity had shifted and I lost my balance easily. Just another hazard of bringing a new life into the world. And I couldn't give our secret away.

But on one knee or not, it wasn't so much about the proposal as the gift and the thought behind it. Jus was going to be so surprised and happy! It was going to be a beautiful thing.

Saturday, December 13th
Justin

It was hard to say what was up with Riggins. Or why he'd been so insistent I tell Kay about *The Nut-cracker*. He brought it up again on Monday when I got into work. Before I'd even opened my first can of energy drink. Don't get me before I've had at least one can, or several cups of coffee. When I pushed back, telling him to butt the hell out, he'd laughed. And given me a knowing look, as if he knew something I didn't.

"Surprises have a way of biting the giver in the butt," he said. "Personally, I don't like surprises. I have it on good authority that this wouldn't be the best time to spring one on Kayla." He gave me a wink-wink-nod-nod kind of look.

I'd frowned at him. "What the hell are you talking about? What do you know that I don't?"

He'd grabbed my energy drink, popped it open, and handed it to me. "You're really slow before your first round of sugar and caffeine in the morning. A word to the wise is all."

I'd been hinting about *The Nutcracker* to Kay through the bracelet and round beads I'd been giving her for advent. My original plan had been to give her the nutcracker bead on the 23rd, and on Christmas Eve a diamond tiara for her to wear to the show.

I didn't see the harm in surprising her. I mean, hell, who else was she going to spend Christmas Eve with? I'd gotten my family's buy-in and hers. They were all keeping it from her. So what was the problem? Who was going to upset my plans?

Riggins thought he knew women so much better than I did. But who was the guy who had the hot blond way out of his league for his wife? Yeah, right, Riggs.

Riggins slapped me on the back. "Women like to know about these kinds of plans ahead of time. So they can make an appointment to have their hair and makeup done. Get a manicure. Find shoes to go with the dress.

"Part of the fun for women is all the pampering and preparation leading up to the event," Riggins had argued. "Do you want to deprive her of that part of the fun? Don't you want her to feel like she looks her best?

"What happens if you surprise her in the middle of a bad hair day? Or right after she comes home sweaty from the gym and needs hours to get ready, not minutes? Whenever you go out, Kayla is going to be in the spotlight and under scrutiny. The public wants a fashion icon. Kayla is now as much the face of Flash as you are. And with an extra dose of pressure to look the part. No, bad plan, my boy.

"Happy women are horny women," he'd said with a grin. "If you don't tell her soon, her hair stylist will be booked. And all the money in the world won't get her an appointment. Just saying."

Damn him. He made a decent point. Maybe a surprise wasn't in my best interest. Maybe the anticipation was part of the fun. So I'd looked around for a romantic, holiday way of springing the surprise on her. And gotten lucky. The annual gingerbread display downtown featured a Nutcracker-themed house. Her mom had told me Kay loved that display. She'd gone almost every year since she was little. First with her parents, then with her friends. And it was time to make my annual appearance, anyway.

I made time to take Saturday off and take her. I would spring my surprise in front of *The Nutcracker* display.

Kayla

Was proposing on the 13th unlucky? I didn't know. But my heart beat out of control as I held Justin's hand and waited in line to get into the gingerbread village. The display was in a hotel lobby, set up so visitors could walk completely around it and see both front and back of the impressive gingerbread buildings. These weren't your run-of-the-mill gingerbread houses. These were massive constructions, some five or six feet tall and half that wide. Lighted, with motors animating parts of the scenes that wrapped around all sides.

More than a display, it was a competition. Each of the eight to ten entries vied for votes, which you texted in. I had never quite figured out what the winner got. All the money raised went to fund juvenile diabetes research. Prestige, maybe? Bragging rights?

A large, clear glass donation box sat at the entrance to the cordoned-off village. You could drop money in or text in your donation. There was no required entry fee, but donations were encouraged. Every year I thought the same thing—you had to see the sense of humor, or irony, or whatever you wanted to call it in concoctions made of sugar and candy raising money for diabetes research.

The hotel lobby sparkled with Christmas decorations and crystal chandeliers. It was a high-end hotel with granite countertops and gold fixtures. The staff dressed in suits. Christmas music played quietly in the background.

While we waited in line, a volunteer came by and passed out candy canes to the children and five-dollar gift cards to a local coffee shop to the adults.

Jus quietly stuffed a hundred-dollar bill in the donation box. If I knew Jus, he hadn't done it to be showy. He'd done it to encourage others to be generous. He had his cellphone in his hand. He turned away for a second. I was sure he'd texted in his generous annual donation.

Our turn came up as the line moved and we inched in front of the display. I smiled as the gingerbread village came into view. Who could be uncheered by the sight of cookie and candy buildings? Every year I felt the same sense of wonder. It was like being a child again, full of candy-cane dreams and magic.

The line moved slowly, as people paused to take pictures and bend down and peer into tiny hard-candy windows. The first house was based on "Santa Claus is Comin' to Town."

"Look, Jus!" I squeezed his hand. "Look at Santa going down the chimney. Do you think he's going to make it?"

Jus grinned. "He's pretty jolly and fat. My bet is not without a hefty dose of Christmas magic."

I bent down to look inside. As well as I could, anyway. It was hard when you had to bend around a baby person at your waist. "There's even soot on the hearth and cookies waiting for him."

Jus leaned beside me, his warm hand on my back.

"Next year you'll get to play Santa," I whispered to him.

"I better start eating cookies now." His eyes twinkled. How merry!

I shook my head and put my hand on his rock-hard abs. "Don't even think about it. I like these the way they are."

So far, we had managed to avoid the paparazzi. Seattle was tolerant of her billionaires, giving them their space and privacy. At least when they were in their regular neighborhood hangouts. But this was a public event that Jus attended every year. An event that would welcome media coverage. Though we hadn't announced our visit ahead of time, we were still fair game. Which added to the thrill, and danger, of proposing to Jus.

I crossed my fingers, hoping to avoid the press entirely.

Jus and I made our way slowly along the row of gingerbread buildings, laughing and commenting on each. Jus tended to comment more on the structural aspects of the designs, marveling at getting a four- or five-story building made out of cookie to stand.

I was in agreement, but for a different reason. "They must control the climate in here. Otherwise, how do these creations not get soggy and collapse? Every gingerbread house I've ever built, even ones made of graham crackers, has gotten soggy and collapsed within days. No matter how crisp it is at first."

I was running off at the mouth, talking about anything to cover my nerves and the pounding of my heart in my ears as we approached the Winter Wonderland display. I hoped Jus didn't notice my anxiety and excitement. Or the way I was trying not to be obvious as I kept an eye out for reporters.

The line started on the backside of the village and wound around to end the tour on the front side of the display. Winter Wonderland was the next-to-last display in the village, giving me time to screw up my courage. But I could hardly wait!

My breath caught when I saw the gingerbread creation. My heart squeezed. It was truly a winter wonderland. A forest of trees on a hill, sparkling with sugary snow and frost. Birds, rabbits, deer, and all manner of forest animals. A quaint cabin in the woods with a roaring fire that actually crackled and lit up. A couple cuddling in front of it. A Christmas tree in the corner. Santa on the roof.

And best of all, a snowman in the yard wearing a clerical collar and a parson's hat. A happy couple kissing in front of him, the bride with a lacy veil made of frost. The groom with rosy cheeks.

"Look!" I said to Jus. "Parson Brown. Isn't that romantic? They've really captured the theme of the song. I always wanted a winter wedding."

He lifted an eyebrow comically. "You did? I thought our summer wedding was perfect." He had that teasing look on his face.

Our "wedding" was an inside joke. Because, of course, I hadn't even been at it. And he didn't remember it.

I rolled my eyes and kissed him lightly. "That was nice. But a winter wedding has always been my secret fantasy. I think this one has my vote. Jus—"

I was just reaching into my purse to hand him my handcrafted, written marriage proposal card, when he grabbed my hand and pulled me forward toward the next display, nearly causing me to topple into him. Being off center and off balance was hell.

"Not so fast!" he said. "You can't vote until you've seen them all." He gave me a crooked, almost boyishly excited grin.

What was going on?

"Wait! I haven't finished looking at this one yet. There's a lot more detail to take in."

"I'm not a fan of that song." He continued pulling me along. "Is it just me or is it dumb to pretend a snowman is a preacher? Who makes a clergyman snowman in the first place? Soldiers, fireman, police, regular old snowmen, the headless snowman—that's a personal favorite—but pastor? Pretend he could marry me to someone?" He shook his head. "Crazy."

"It's romantic and whimsical in its way." I tried to resist moving on, but Jus was too strong and insistent.

"Look at this! Now *this* is a classic." He squeezed my hand. "Huh? Good, isn't it? Fairies. Pink spun sugar. Dancing peacocks. Princes. Soldiers. Christmas trees. Representatives from nations of the world?" He glanced at me for confirmation.

I thought he was overselling it. Then I took a closer look. "*The Nutcracker!* Oh, it *is* nice. I love *The Nutcracker.*"

I forgot myself, and my mission, as I took in the intricate detail of this entry in the competition.

It was good. It was better than good. It was beautiful. Complicated. Evocative.

"Oh, look! There's the Sugar Plum Fairy! And there!" I pointed. "Clara in front of the Christmas tree." I leaned in for a closer look. "Is this based on the new Ian Falconer set?"

Justin's eyes danced. "It is. Kay, how would—"

Just then, a little boy, no more than four, pushed between us, squealing at an earsplitting volume as he tried to get away from his dad.

"Get back here, tiger." His dad broke between us. "Sorry." He looked harried as he flashed us an apologetic smile. "He's a fast one. You turn your head for one second and they run away." He looked at my belly and laughed. "You'll find out soon enough."

As he picked up his son, the boy burst into an even louder round of screams and protests.

Jus, who was normally good-natured and patient with anything having to do with children, looked irritated at the interruption.

He squeezed my hand. "This one gets my vote."

"Not so fast." I looked around again to make sure there were no reporters. "It is definitely nice. But we have to see the front side of the others before we decide. Those are your rules, not mine," I teased.

"Damn the rules. I made them. I can change them," he said. "I like this one." He reached into his pocket, ostensibly to pull out his phone, as I reached into my purse for the card.

I was half expecting him to pull out my advent charm bracelet bead of the day instead of his phone. Which, of course, would be another Nutcracker bead. Explaining his excitement and why he wanted me to vote for this particular display. He was so undeniably adorable and romantic. This was threatening to be the best bead presentation yet.

But I was losing ground and getting nervous I was going to blow my opportunity. I had to get my surprise in before we moved away from wonderland entry. Or we got another unexpected interruption.

We spoke at the same time.

"I've been trying to find the perfect way to give you this." Puzzlingly, he pulled neither his phone nor a small jewelry box out. Instead, he pulled an envelope from his pocket with a flourish and held it out to me. "I had to pull all kinds of strings—"

I pulled the marriage proposal card from my purse and looked deep into his eyes as I went up on my toes and whispered in his ear. "I have something for you, too."

I took the envelope from him. He took the card from me.

"You first!" we said in unison again. "No, you!"

"Jinx!" I finally said.

"All right, clearly, great minds think alike. We'll open them together." His gaze held mine. "Agreed?"

I nodded. "Agreed."

The envelope he'd handed me was unsealed and looked like a ticket sleeve. I opened the flap and pulled out eight tickets to *The Nutcracker*. Box seats. And a note in Justin's neat engineering printing. *A new tradition for the whole family. Both sides are going. Your parents. My parents and brothers. You and me.*

I stopped reading and gave a girly squeal. "Jus!"

Jus had opened the handmade card I'd given him and was staring at it with a shocked, still expression.

I held my breath. I'd taken great pains with the calligraphy and the wording. I'd spent an inordinate amount of time stamping, cutting out shapes, and applying appliques, embossing, and even glitter, using every card-making technique I knew. I'd used my design skills and premium, high-quality cardstock, sparing no expense. I'd even judiciously applied gold and silver foil to make a Christmas wedding announcement/marriage proposal card. And though the calligraphy wasn't as pretty as a professional's, it got my point across.

I watched his face as he silently read the words I'd penned.

Kayla Marie Lucas Green invites you, Justin Arnold Green, love of her life, fake husband, father-to-be of her child, and lover, to really *marry her, in a legitimate, legal ceremony, sanctioned by the State of New York, complete with a genuine, authentic, and legally binding second marriage license on December 24th at 1 p.m. in New York State. We won't be married by a snowman. But the preacher's name is Brown.*

This was where I had planned to whisper in his ear, *Will you* really *marry me, Jus?*

Instead, I was staring at the date on *The Nutcracker* tickets. And the rest of his note. *It will be a Christmas Eve to remember.*

It *certainly* would.

Before either of us could speak—it was safe to say we were both speechless with surprise—a camera flashed, immortalizing the moment and our stunned expressions. My sometimes ally, sometimes nemesis, local daytime TV personality and talk show host Sunshine Sheri, appeared with a camera crew in tow.

I'd been so absorbed in this beautiful, bittersweet fiasco of a moment, I hadn't noticed her come in.

Who invited her? I thought. And what was she doing, lurking behind a potted palm, waiting to pounce on us?

Before we could turn and run, her eyes lit with a predatory glint. She smiled an evil, slow smile of satisfaction. The ball on her red Santa hat bounced. Of course she was wearing a Santa hat! Her heels clicked on the polished granite floor, the sound of my beautiful marriage proposal being interrupted and ruined. And I swore her crew had moved into position to block all the exits.

She hurried toward us with a cheery wave, parting the crowd waiting to get into the holiday gingerbread village as easily as Mrs. Claus herself. A whisper of excitement rippled through the line as people recognized one of the city's perkiest daytime personalities.

We're going to be on TV!

People pointed and waved to the cameras. A few even shamelessly held their babies up. And waved their little hands, pimping them out to get noticed. Babies always caught the eye. And this display was for the children.

As the cameras panned the line of people, I contemplated the odds that I could outrun her crew. Jus and I were probably the only two people who did *not* want to be caught on TV. And yet we were clearly her quarry.

"Sheri! Sheri!" The people reached for her.

Sheri was in her element, shaking hands, smiling, waving. She was thin, an aging beauty of the news anchor ilk. She wore a red sweater and black belt. Black slacks and boots. Her blond hair fell to her shoulders in waves beneath that Santa hat.

Her career had been revived, in part thanks to Jus marrying me. Long story.

"If it isn't Justin and Kayla Green!" she gushed as she reached us, as if the meeting was *totally* accidental. A happy coincidence.

Right.

"Let's just see if we can catch them for a moment!" She held her forefinger half an inch from her thumb. She waved to us again. "Tell us, Justin and Kayla, how fabulous is the display this year? And for such a worthy cause!"

Oh, crap.

CHAPTER NINE

Kayla

As Sunshine Sheri approached, Jus grabbed me and pulled me close. "Yes," he whispered without hesitation or question. He looked at me with his heart in his eyes. "I'll really marry you." He gave me a quick kiss to seal the deal. "We'll work it out."

It was so like Jus to save the moment, and me from total humiliation. I'd been hoping for more time. More passion. A long, lingering kiss. But no one could deny the intimacy of that instant between us.

He slid the card I'd given him into his pocket just as Sheri reached us.

"Justin Green! You're such a big supporter of children's causes. I was *hoping* we'd catch you on your annual visit to the gingerbread houses," Sheri said.

"Second Saturday of December three years running now. Am I right?"

Jus grimaced ever so slightly. Obviously kicking himself for being so predictable. But who but Sunshine Sheri would have paid attention to his gingerbread visiting habits?

"Good to see you, Sheri." He leaned forward and hugged her like she was an old friend.

Jus was always gracious and welcoming. Genuine in an affectionate way people loved and appreciated.

I was glad the focus was on him, because right at that moment I was trying hard not to scowl. And losing. Back to the naughty list for me.

"And it's delicious to see my favorite billionaire." She took his hands and squeezed them.

I was dazed and disappointed as I stood next to Jus, holding *The Nutcracker* tickets like a reindeer in the headlights.

"Kayla!" Sheri held her arms open to me.

Damn. There was nothing to do but hug her.

Wrong thing. Wrong *move*.

Sheri spotted the tickets. "What's this?" She caught my hand and looked at them. "*Nutcracker* tickets! Those are *impossible* to get. It sold out in, what? September?" She looked to Jus for confirmation.

He shrugged.

"And for Christmas Eve. Now, you have to have clout to get those." She wiggled her eyebrows and mugged for the camera. "What an absolutely thoughtful gesture!"

Crap! Now we're trapped.

Oblivious to the drama playing out between Jus and me, Sheri glanced at the display we were standing in front of and back to Justin.

"You are just the most *adorable* billionaire!" She stared right at the rolling camera. "Isn't he, girls? Did you just surprise Kayla with those tickets? Right here in front of the Nutcracker gingerbread display? See!"

She leaned toward the camera, confidentially speaking to it. "This is why we love Justin, isn't it, ladies? Top of the nice list for him!"

I was feeling sick as Sheri turned to me. And beating myself up for being slow and stupid and too stunned to think. If I'd thought as quickly on my feet as Jus had, those tickets would be safely out of sight in my purse.

"The Greens are going to *The Nutcracker* on Christmas Eve! What a special way to celebrate."

She'd been sickeningly bright and perky before. Now she was downright glowing and positively annoying. "We'll be there, too! Special Christmas Eve coverage. Interviewing people. We'll be looking for you. You'll have to stop and say hello and wish our audience merry Christmas!"

I felt sick. My slow reaction time may have just blown any chance of a Christmas Eve wedding. And after Jus had just tried to save it.

"You'd better keep your eye on Justin, Kayla," Sheri said. "After this romantic gesture, girls are going to want him even more. If you ever let him go, there will be a line of girls waiting to snap him up!"

"I'm not planning on losing him anytime soon. Anytime *period.*" I put my arm around him, possessive.

Jus looped his arm me, beaming. He had the same grin on his face he'd had when I told him I loved him the first time. Awe. Wonder. Complete happiness.

I felt the same way. If only I hadn't been so stupid and slow...

"Do you have a favorite display this year?" Sheri asked him. "Do we have to guess? Or does it start with *The Nutcracker*?" She laughed as she winked into the camera.

"Winter Wonderland," Jus said without hesitating. He pulled out his phone. "I'm texting my vote in right now. I've always loved that bit about the snowman and Parson Brown. Look at that snowman and tell me they haven't captured it perfectly."

"Liar!" I mouthed to him.

He winked and turned the conversation away from us to what a worthy charity this village was raising money for, encouraging everyone to visit it and donate.

Justin

I've had my share of fantasies. Since freshman year of college, most of them regarding Kay. But never in my wildest dreams did I imagine *her* proposing to *me*. It was enough of a stretch to imagine her accepting my proposal.

I finally managed to extricate us from Sunshine Sheri's grasp. "Merry Christmas! Happy holidays! You'll have to excuse us now, Sheri. We have a busy day of Christmas shopping ahead. Only twelve days until Christmas. Busy, busy, busy!"

"You don't do all of your shopping through Flashionista?" Sheri asked.

I winked at her. "Not *all*."

She signaled "cut" to the cameras.

"Thanks for humoring me," Sheri said to us when they were no longer on us. "We got some good footage. This should bring people down. We'll be airing this segment on Monday's show."

I nodded. "Great! We'll be watching for it. Really, nice to see you, Sheri. Happy holidays!"

I grabbed Kay's hand and pulled her past the crew and gathering crowds into the revolving door.

"We could go round and round for fun." I winked at her.

She shook her head, laughing. Damn, I liked seeing her happy. "This isn't *Elf*."

"We need to watch that movie." I pulled her out onto the sidewalk, into the noise of the street and the city. "I love you!"

Delirious with joy, I threw my arms around her, wide baby belly and all. Picked her up off her feet beneath her butt, holding her so that she towered above me, and lifted my face for a kiss.

She cupped my face. "I love you, too. You're happy?"

"Ecstatic!" I mugged for a kiss again.

She laughed and lowered her lips to mine, kissing me in that sweet, hot way that made me want to take her in the street. That made my heart sing and my pulse race.

Someone walked by and yelled at us, "Hey! Where's the mistletoe?"

I spun her around, still kissing her. When I stopped, she was breathless.

She smiled down at me. "Your kisses are positively dizzying!"

"Yeah?" I grinned. I couldn't stop grinning. "I have that effect on women. It's my animal magnetism."

"Ah," she said. "I thought it was the spinning. But that explains it." She laughed. "Now put me down. People are staring at us."

"Let them stare!" I laughed, too. The sun was shining. It was a beautiful, cold, clear December day. But even if it had been raining, it would have been a gorgeous day.

"Jus!"

I shook my head and set her gently on her feet. "I *love* you. In more ways than you'll ever know."

"Really?" she said. "Let me count the ways—"

I grabbed her fingers and kissed them. "Your hands are cold." I pulled my gloves from my coat pocket. "Wear mine."

She pulled a pair for her pocket and held them up. "I have my own. But you're sweet."

"You've made me the happiest guy in the world."

"In the world?" Her eyes sparkled.

With tears of joy, I hoped.

"I love you, too."

The way she said it, softly, deeply, made my heart sing. "Say it again?"

"What?" She looked puzzled. "I love you?"

I grinned. "Yeah. Say it a million times. I never get tired of hearing it."

She shook her head. "You're crazy. And way too easy to please."

I grabbed her hand and pulled her down the street.

She looked at me quizzically. "Where are we going?"

"Somewhere you can tell me all about it. Everything. I want to hear all about our wedding plans." I stopped suddenly, pulling her up short in front of me. "We can really get married in New York? With a genuine second license? That we both sign? I thought that wasn't legal anywhere in the US."

She tenderly stroked my beard, laughing, I presumed at my enthusiasm. "Yes, we can really get married. You and me. Not you and some imposter." She paused, turning suddenly serious.

"Jus, I never got to say the words. I was going to actually ask you to marry me. I rehearsed and everything."

"So say them now."

She glanced around at the people walking by. "Out on the street? I feel silly."

"Kay?" I coaxed.

"Justin Arnold—"

"I hate that middle name."

She gave me the look.

"Sorry." I put on an apologetic face. "Proceed."

"Justin Arnold Green, will you *really* marry *me*?" She tapped her chest. "Not a fake. Not a proxy. But really marry *me*?"

"Yes!" I kissed her again, deeply, lingering. Shit, I loved the way she kissed me, running her tongue over my lips until I trembled. Nibbling me. Pressing up against me.

She pulled away suddenly. "Jus, what *are* we going to do? In our rush to surprise each other, we've booked competing events. And now that Sunshine Sheri has announced our attendance at *The Nutcracker* to the world—"

"We'll cancel," I said. "Give our tickets away. I'd rather marry you any day."

She pursed her lips. "Jus, how much trouble did you go to to get these tickets?"

"Riggins—" I started to say.

"Riggins!" she said at the same time.

We stared at each other in surprise.

"You, too?" we said together.

"We have to stop this speaking-in-unison crap." Her hand was still cold. I tucked it in my pocket with mine. "I want to hear everything. But not out here on the street. I have an idea!" I let go of her hand, pulled out my phone, made an online reservation, and called for a cab. "Come on!"

"Where are we going?"

I grinned. "Someplace private. In the mood for a Ferris wheel ride?"

Kayla

Less than fifteen minutes later, we were being escorted to the front of the line at the wheel, each carrying a T-shirt to commemorate the moment. Jus had paid for two consecutive rides, which was good for about forty minutes of complete, private alone time.

"You two look happy," the attendant said as he opened the door to the private VIP gondola. "Having a good time downtown?"

Jus grinned. "Oh, yeah."

Then we were locked in, cuddled together on the leather seat as the gondola rose and people boarded the next gondola below us. It was just the two of us. With soft Christmas music playing in the background and a view of the city decorated for the holidays before us.

"This is perfect! Date day on the wheel like all the high school and college kids? And tourists!" I teased.

He was grinning ear to ear. "Hey, it's private. We have the T-shirts." He flashed four champagne toast drink coupons. "And we can have a holiday toast later."

I shook my head and patted my baby bump. "Am I allowed?"

He put his arm around me. "So talk. Tell me everything. I want to know all the details of my upcoming real wedding to you. New York? This is really legit? How did you find out about it?"

As the wheel went up and around, we took in the view of the city, the sound, and the mountains. I told him everything, all the details. "A lunch conversation with my sorority sister Kelly put me on to it. She was telling me about her friend's secret wedding and all the headaches involved." I gave him the details and took him through my discovery process.

"So I looked into it, and sure enough, New York will issue a second license under specific circumstances." I listed them for him.

He squeezed my hand, beaming. He hadn't stopped smiling. He looked as elated as if he'd proposed and this had been our real engagement. "Why do I feel like shouting this out to the world? I'm really going to marry this girl!" He held our clasped hands up in a victory-type pose.

"Shut up!" I leaned my head on his shoulder.

"I want to tell everyone. Not kidding. This is brilliant. You're brilliant. I'd been thinking of surprising you on our first anniversary with a recommitment ceremony some place romantic. Maybe Italy. So you could have the dream ceremony you always wanted and our family and friends could celebrate with us. But I couldn't find any way to get another completely legal license and marriage certificate. You've outplayed me!"

"Well, of course, I *am* a genius. Which is why you married me," I joked, playfully bumping him with my shoulder. "I can't believe, though, that I'm acing myself out of the dream wedding ceremony."

"Who says we can't have a recommitment ceremony for family and friends next year anyway?"

He was so damn cute when he was excited. "Maybe. After I get my figure back."

"You'll get it back." He kissed me. "Even if you don't, you'll still be beautiful. Now, tell me about the ceremony."

"I've booked a little private wedding chapel on the banks of the Hudson River in upstate New York for

Christmas Eve day, just like the invitation says. I have a pastor, whose name really is Brown, James Brown, just like I wrote."

"That was no joke?"

"Not at all." I answered all of his questions. Telling him about the rules for New York weddings. How I'd had his tux cleaned. And Harry had gotten the twenty-four-hour waiting period waiver. How the marriage records would be sealed and not part of the public record.

As the icing on it all, I brought out the postnup prenup I'd had Harry draw up and I'd signed. I handed it to Jus, wrapped in a bow.

His brow furrowed. "What's this?"

"Another present." I bit my lip. "To show you that all I want is you. Not your money. Just your love. And that you have all of mine."

He untied the ribbon and pulled out the legal document, skimming it. As he read, the furrow in his brow deepened. "A prenup?"

I nodded. "It's your basic postnuptial prenup, giving me a fixed sum of ten million, as we had originally agreed. So I didn't think you'd object to the amount. Though it can be changed if you like. Anyway, should we ever...split, which we won't, the amount will be adjusted for inflation for the duration of our marriage. And half of any joint assets we accumulate after our marriage. Which, because we're a community property state, is Washington State law. That part can't be altered.

"But read it at your leisure." I winked at him. "And have your lawyer look it over. Since he drafted it—"

Jus tossed it back in my lap. "I'm not signing that."

"Jus, I want this done right. You should have had a prenup when you originally fake-married me. That was part of the reason for our ruse in the first place, to protect you from being taken to the cleaners.

"As your current fake wife, I would advise you to protect yourself and your assets. You've earned your billions. I don't want them, not if I don't have you to go with them. I don't want you to ever doubt that I love you."

His Adam's apple bobbed. His eyes got misty. He hugged me to him.

"Please, Jus. Sign it for me. But do it at Harry's office where it can be witnessed and notarized so it will be legal."

"One hundred million and not a penny less."

I stared at him.

"You get one hundred million or I won't sign. That's a pittance of my net worth." He was using his hard-ass negotiating voice. Which meant he wouldn't budge.

I sighed and extended my hand for a shake. "Deal. But you know it's not what I want."

He shook. "Deal." Then he frowned again. "Is a postnuptial prenuptial even a thing? Even legal?"

I shrugged. "Harry's not sure. There's no case law. But why wouldn't it be? People renegotiate contracts all the time."

He kissed me. "Damn, Kay, I love you."

"I love you, too." I stared into his eyes. "But what are we going to do now? We have to be at the Christmas Eve *Nutcracker*. And that's when I've booked our wedding!"

Then I thought of Riggins and I smiled. "I was mad at Riggins for strong-arming me into telling you early. I was going to surprise you with this the morning of the 23rd. Now I see his point."

"Riggins knows about the wedding?" Justin's smile disappeared.

"Not about the wedding. Just that I wanted to take you away for Christmas Eve and Christmas Day. I had to let him in on that much. I needed his help. He agreed to cover for you at Flash and the children's hospital on the 24th.

"What about you? What was Riggins' involvement in the *Nutcracker* surprise?"

Jus sighed. "He was instrumental in getting me the tickets. And he insisted I tell you, too, claiming surprises could backfire." Jus shook his head and grinned.

We laughed together at that.

"Okay, so we give Riggins points for being sneaky, but a good friend.

"But what do we do now? I didn't think you'd want to be away from Flash during peak. I assumed the bulk of everything would be done by Christmas Eve. We would tell our family we were busy and wanted to be alone on our first Christmas and sneak off and get married.

"For most people, getting married on Christmas Eve is a bad deal. Your anniversary on another holiday for life?" I shook my head. "Not so romantic. Except for us. We'll always be able to sneak an anniversary present in with the rest."

"You thought of everything," Jus said.

"Except you surprising me." I grimaced. "And putting those tickets away before Sheri saw them."

"I hate to say this—this is the best surprise of my life, other than when I convinced you to fake-marry me and I hate to mess with it—can we postpone the wedding until after Christmas?"

I really hated to tell him this part. I was hoping to avoid it until after Christmas. I sighed and shook my head. "I'm grounded after Christmas. Remember that spotting I had earlier this month? Add to that I'm at risk for going into preterm labor, and my doctor wants to err on the side of caution. She reluctantly gave me permission to fly until Christmas."

He stared at me with a worried expression and laid his hand on my baby bump. "Why didn't you tell me? Is she going to be okay? Are you—"

"We're both fine. Everything's fine. The doctor is just being cautious."

"We'll get married in the next twelve days—"

Guys! They were such fixers. But this couldn't be fixed.

I shook my head. "One, with the port strike on top of peak, that would put too much stress and pressure on you. Let's face it, it just wouldn't look good to the investors and would be bad for Flash and employee morale. You can't ask them to put in long hours and then go dancing off on vacation, even for a day." I was thinking more and more like an entrepreneur every minute.

"Two, how would we convince Riggins? And three, even if all that were possible, there are no venues, nothing available. Everything is booked. I was lucky to get something on Christmas Eve. And only then because most of the wedding venues are empty. Most people aren't crazy enough to get married on December 24th. Especially when it's midweek."

"We'll make it possible. We'll get married at the courthouse." Jus nodded, agreeing with his own point and ignoring the rest of mine. "It won't be as romantic. But if the idea is just to get legitimately married—"

"It is!" I said. "And I wish it were that simple. But the only way to get a second license is if the celebrant requires one to conduct the ceremony. And in New York, you get your license at town hall, not the courthouse. Anyway, the town clerk won't conduct a second ceremony because the state considers it a recommitment ceremony, not a marriage. I checked."

His face fell.

"I know!" I said. "It makes no sense. They'll issue a second license if a member of the clergy requires one for a second ceremony. But they won't conduct one. And, at this late date, just try to find a celebrant who will perform the ceremony before Christmas, require the license, and doesn't mind conducting it on a tarmac because there are no venues—"

He squeezed my shoulders. "You're right. It was shitty of me to even suggest it. After all the trouble you've gone to to surprise me and plan a real wedding against all the odds, we're getting married on December 24th at the little chapel on the Hudson River in New York State by Parson Brown."

"Sounds like a game of Clue," I said.

"Babe"—he took my chin and tipped my face up to his—"I would marry you anytime anywhere again and again. We're going to do this." He sounded suddenly fierce and determined.

"We'll fly out the 23rd after the Santa Sample Sale, get the license, get married at one, which is only ten in the morning Seattle time. The ceremony will be quick. No reception. Okay, correct that. One on the jet on the way back, just between you and me." He gave me a lecherous look.

I raised an eyebrow and laughed. "You and me and my cousin Dex, if we can convince him. We need a witness. Fortunately, just one, not two like here. He's the only other person who knows about us, so tag, he's it. We just have to convince him to give up his Christmas Eve day for us."

Justin's eyes lit up. He brushed my worry about Dex aside. "Dex will jump at the chance to do something different for a change."

"To fly five hours across the country and back?"

"We'll make it worth his while. I have ways of convincing him. Bargaining chips. Leave it to me." Jus paused. "Back to logistics. It's a five-hour flight. Less on a business jet, especially if we catch the winds. Going west home we gain, rather than lose, three hours. We can be back on the plane by eleven our time. Home by four.

"Dex makes it back for Christmas Eve dinner. We're at the ballet by seven thirty. It will be tight."

"But doable," I added. "I love you." I bit my lip. "Let's hope nothing else comes up to get in our way."

I held out my hand. "And don't you have something else for me? Like my advent bead? I thought that's what you were going to give me at the gingerbread houses."

He grinned and reached into another pocket. "You're terrible."

"And greedy," I said with a smile.

CHAPTER TEN

Monday, December 15th

Kayla

I was in my office on my computer working on details for the Santa Sample Sale when my mom called.

"I just saw you and Justin on Sunshine Sheri's show!"

Mom was always delighted when I made it on TV. She was a successful lawyer, but somehow the sight of her only child on TV made her day and gave her bragging rights. Her girl was famous! Her thoughts, not mine.

"I'm glad Justin told you about the ballet! I was bursting keeping it to myself. He called us early last week to invite us. Those tickets are impossible to get!

Even for a billionaire, I would imagine." She sounded impressed.

Almost everything about Jus impressed her.

"We're all lucky to have Justin in the family. He's such a thoughtful young man. I appreciate him trying to accommodate both mothers and give all of us equal family time."

She paused and I sensed a "but" coming.

"I suppose that's the downside of having a married daughter. There's that other family to consider and share you with.

"It's just...you're our only child. And they have two other sons. Who, by your account, are their favorites. You'd think they could give a little and let you spend *all* of Christmas Eve with us. I'm not so sure about sharing a box at the ballet with the Greens. They'll outnumber us."

I'd been murmuring my agreement as she talked. My mind mostly elsewhere, occupied with making sure we were fulfilling as many Christmas wishes at the sample sale as possible.

"You like the Greens, Mom. You said so yourself."

"Mmmmmm," she said, obviously hedging. "What I know of them. But it *is* a little awkward when we first meet, as it is with people who aren't well acquainted. I think the thing is we never got to get to know them properly during an engagement period and wedding season. Eloping on the spur of the moment like you did—"

"Saved you a lot of headaches. Think how it could have been—fighting over who gets to invite who and sit where and pay for what. You should be grateful," I teased her. "And shouldn't you be working?"

"We're recessed for lunch," she said. "Well, anyway, I hope Justin won't mind a few family pictures. Just of our family. Not that I'm averse to a *few* with the Greens, too. But you know how I like my Christmas Eve family photos. And you will be spending the night with us?"

"Actually, I was thinking this year you and Dad, and the Greens, should all come spend the night here with us. We have a big house and plenty of room—"

"Kayla!"

"Teasing, Mom. Though you and Dad could come spend the night with us. We have three trees."

"Yeesss, but that won't seem like Christmas, will it? Tradition!"

"Things are changing, Mom. I'll humor you this year, but next year is a whole new game."

"That's generous of you, child." She laughed. "I suppose it could be worse. My sister called. She's unhappy with her headstrong only child, your cousin Dex. Well, who else?" She laughed at herself.

"Anyway, he's going on some kind of overnight snowboarding trip with friends on the 23rd and won't be home until dinner on Christmas Eve."

I held my tongue and tried not to laugh. Jus had done his job and talked Dex into being our witness. I didn't know what Jus had promised him, but I would bet whatever it was was good. My aunt, my mom's twin sister, would be furious at me if she knew I was the source behind Dex's trip. Given the circumstances, though, what could I do?

"Are you sniggering?" Mom said.

Oops! Not doing such a good job at holding it in.

"It's not funny," she said.

"No, Mom. But it's *exactly* like Dex."

Yes, I threw my cousin who was doing me a Christmas favor under the bus. Evil, evil. Well, he'd pranked me enough during my lifetime that he probably deserved it. And was being handsomely compensated for his effort, I was sure.

"You have a point!" Mom laughed, too. "Before I forget. I've been meaning to ask you. I haven't done my baking yet."

Which was *exactly* like Mom every year. She was a perpetually late, last-minute baker. At least her cookies were always fresh on Christmas Eve and she didn't have to pull them out of the freezer, either.

"Can you come over on the 23rd and make cookies with me? We'll have so much fun! We'll send your dad out and watch Christmas movies while we bake..." She kept talking, selling it with as much enthusiasm as if she was on the shopping channel.

I had stopped listening. *Crap.* No matter how much holiday time I gave her, it was just like Mom to angle for more and put me on the spot.

Think fast, I told myself. *Think up a lie and think it up quick!*

"Kayla?"

"Sorry, Mom. I can't. Jus and I have plans on the 23rd." I crossed my fingers, hoping she wouldn't pry.

"Plans." Her voice fell. "That's nice." She was really trying to rally and make allowances now that I was a married woman. "Unfortunately, the 23rd is the only time I can do it. What are you up to that night? Can it be moved?"

If she'd known I was flying to my real wedding, she would have been horrified she'd asked.

"No. Sorry. I've planned a special date night," I lied. Sort of. I couldn't very well tell her I was going to make Jus her actual son-in-law. Yes, Jus was going to be real, too! Wait. Wasn't that the Pinocchio story?

"Two days before Christmas?" Her voice dripped suspicion. She was probably thinking I was putting her off.

Which I was, in a way.

"Jus and I have barely had *any* time together this holiday season. Which is my favorite time of year. *Peak*!" I said with enough disdain to sound like the Grinch.

"Ah, yes, the infamous peak." She chuckled. "I *suppose* you deserve some time together before Christmas." She was clearly trying to be supportive, but she sounded disappointed all the same.

"Well," she said, changing the subject with a filler word. Typical for her. "Have you seen the ten-day weather forecast? It doesn't look like we're going to get a white Christmas this year."

What else was new? We seldom did. I'd lived in the Seattle area all my life and could only remember a few.

"They're predicting mild, pleasant weather. It would serve your mountain-going cousin right if there was no snow for this snowboarding trip of his! They're predicting a terrible year for the ski resorts."

Uh-oh. Mountain snow, where are you when I need you to provide Dex an alibi? Problems, problems.

"The East Coast, though!" Mom was saying. "Brrrr. They're expecting a blizzard. I wouldn't want to be in New York State over Christmas, that's for sure! Remember that storm they had that shut New York City down a few years ago? This could be that bad, or worse. So they're saying.

"The meteorologists are already warning New Yorkers to get their holiday shopping done early. They'll have a white Christmas for sure. I just hope Rudolph can get Santa's sleigh through."

My heart thudded to a dead stop. Fixing Dex's cover story was a small problem. But a big snowstorm could derail my whole wedding. "What?"

"Not like it matters to us!" She paused. "Anyway, they're often wrong. Especially this far out. But they like to be sensational, don't they? Oops! Look at the time. I have to run. Recess is over. Talk to you soon!"

After scaring me with dire warnings of an epic New York snow, she cut me off and went back to court. I hoped she was right about them being wrong. About New York. I looked up the weather for my New York destination wedding. And yes, she was correct about the weather report. New York was bracing for the storm of the century.

Fortunately, the century is young, I told myself. *Maybe it won't be so bad.*

"Oh, crap!" I said, not believing myself. Another thing to worry about.

I called Jus and worried to him, poor guy. Like he needed another stress in his hectic life. Or a pregnant, panicked bride-to-be on his hands.

"Nothing to worry about! They're never right this far out. If they're predicting a blizzard it will probably be fifty and sunny that day."

He was completely nonchalant and unconcerned. Almost too indifferent to chances of impending wedding-cancelling weather.

"We won't have Rudolph the Red-Nosed Reindeer," I said. "We'll have to hope our plane blinks like a blinking beacon to light the way."

Jus laughed. "Both the jet and the airport we're flying into are rated for all weather conditions. A little snow won't stop us."

His confidence was almost reassuring. "Almost" being the key word. I wasn't the bravest flyer anyway.

Friday, December 19th
Justin

Kay had planned a beautiful executive party. Our house looked festive. Kay looked even better. My gaze followed her around as she effortlessly mingled, charmed, and made small talk with the execs and top management from Flash.

Riggins had hosted the party last year. This year, now that I was living in a house, not a bachelor place, it was my turn. I was grateful to have a hostess as efficient and beautiful as Kay. She made the party sparkle.

I wasn't adept at small talk. Not like Kay. Our dog, Data, had been locked out of the way in another part of the house. In a room without a tree. She wasn't certain about the trees and ornaments and had a habit of attacking anything that jingled.

Too bad for Data. She would have loved licking up the delicious crumbs. And been pampered and lavished with attention. She was a Pomsky, a Husky/Pomeranian mix that made for a dog about as cute as they got.

It wasn't supposed to be a night for business, but Flash, and the storms pummeling the East Coast, was on everyone's mind. I was soon locked in conversation with Darren, Paul, and Barry. My heads of transportation, procurement, and facilities. They'd borne the biggest brunt of the port strike and now the storm.

Fortunately, Kay was across the room talking with some of the ladies from merchandising and photography. I didn't want her to pick up on my concerns about the storm.

I got lost deep in a discussion on the problems facing us.

Paul shook his head. "This latest snowstorm is killing us, Justin. With the West Coast ports closed and our guaranteed in-time-for-Christmas delivery, we're being killed.

"I anticipated an upswing in orders, and ordered enough shipping boxes and bags to accommodate it. But we've had record orders. We're running short. Usually, it's a good problem to have. But with the ports closed, I can't get any more in from China. Not in time." He paused.

"Kayla's done a beautiful job here." He looked around the room. "Damn hard to enjoy the festivities with this storm hanging over our heads. I have my feelers out for domestic packaging material manufacturers, begging for any inventory they have. But it won't be branded in the Flash colors with the Flash logo. And we're going to have to pay dearly for it."

He sipped his drink. "Everyone's in the same boat. Demand is high and suppliers can name their price. They're raking it in."

Darren looked glum and serious, too. "The port strike!" He snorted. "As if that wasn't bad enough, the snow on the ground in the east is hampering our carriers. The storms are rolling in every thirty-six hours, dumping more snow. And the big one is still scheduled for late Christmas Eve. If we don't have everything delivered by about three in the afternoon, we're out of luck. And it's going to cost us."

The guys went suddenly quiet.

Darren smiled at someone over my shoulder. "Great party, Kayla! The boss clearly married up. I've never had food this good at any of his parties."

I turned and found Kay standing at my elbow, pale, but forcing a smile.

"Thank you." Her eyes found mine. She was clearly worried.

I caught her later, after the party was over, and the caterers had cleaned up and cleared out. "You must be exhausted. Get some rest."

She had circles beneath her eyes. "Are you coming to bed?"

I shook my head. "Not yet. I have work to do." More work to do than there were hours in the day.

She touched my arm. "Jus, why didn't you tell me? How bad are things?"

I shrugged. "No more challenging than any other holiday season."

She gave me a look of disbelief. "Don't lie to me."

"I'm not." I caught her by the arms. "It's always something. That's what makes this business exciting. If it were easy, what fun would it be?"

"People aren't going to be happy with you taking Christmas Eve off, are they? I thought by then—"

"By then it won't matter. I'll have done everything I can. It will all be in the hands of the local delivery services."

She stared up at me. "But the storms, Jus. They're real now and they aren't letting up. What if we can't make it to New York?"

"We're still five days out. A lot can change in five days. Let's not think about 'what if' tonight. You heard the guys. The height of the storm isn't supposed to hit until late afternoon. We'll be married and long gone by then. Home in Seattle where the skies are gray, the trees are always green, and the Christmases almost never white." I hugged her to me. "It'll be fine. We'll be legally married by Christmas morning."

I sounded more confident than I felt. I didn't want to let her down. I would give her anything in my power.

But there were some things money couldn't buy. The weather's cooperation was, unfortunately, one of them.

CHAPTER ELEVEN

Tuesday, December 23rd
Kayla
The packages were laid in the sample sale wish list fulfillment section with care, in hopes that their buyers soon would be there. Labeled and ready to be purchased and wrapped and put beneath a tree.

My Santa Sample Sale volunteer elves were in position, wearing Santa hats and light-up Christmas bulb necklaces so bright you could even say they glowed.

One corner of the room looked like Santa's workshop, filled with samples of toys Flash had offered in their famous flash sales all fall. Toys and gadgets children were begging for.

There were boxes of glittering holiday costume jewelry and everyday jewelry, some small and dainty, some

large and showy. Hoards of purses and accessories. I
had my eye out for one with a kiss-lock closure. Boxes
of clothes, clearly marked by size. Racks of holiday
dresses that caught the light like the moon on new fall-
en snow. Dresses perfect for Christmas Eve or New
Year's. There were stacks of small appliances and
household items. Gifts, perfect gifts for everyone!

The big conference room at Flash had been turned
into a holiday garage sale with the best bargains in the
city on stylish boutique apparel and jewelry, state-of-
the-art gadgets, and finds for the person with discrim-
inating taste, or plain old quirky style.

I'd always thought shopping at one of the nearly
monthly Flash sample sales was a combination of a
treasure hunt and a garage sale, except everything was
brand new and in style. All the goods belonged in a
classy department store, but usually there was none of
the high-end ambience here. No gently playing piano
music. No wafts of delicate perfume. No perfectly arranged displays or showcased items. No well-lit dressing rooms and helpful salespeople. The same items, but
at prices that made them total steals.

Amazing how atmosphere and a good display influ-
enced a buyer's perception of quality and the shopping
experience. It was a psychology I'd studied in college.
Which is why I'd had the room perfumed with the
scents of Christmas—fir forest, cinnamon, and spice.
Borrowed props from the studio to decorate and add
holiday cheer. And set up a temporary dressing room in
the back. It still wasn't the mall. But it was nice.
Christmas piano music even played in the background.

Time and again, I was overwhelmed by the clutter of the sample sales and magnitude of the jumbled goods and the search. While pawing through boxes, nothing seemed as beautiful and valuable as it was. Until you got it home and put it on or laid it out. Then you realized the bargain you'd gotten.

I was trying to create that sense of a treasure hunt for the employee shoppers today. Trying to add a bit of Christmas and holiday shopping atmosphere by playing soft music in the background and setting up the wish fulfillment center.

This sale was the best one of the year and one of the perks of working at Flash. I wanted it to be special and fun. For shoppers to come away with an experience. Happy with their purchases and eager to give them as the exceptional gifts they were.

Did it matter to the receiver of a hundred-dollar crystal necklace that it only cost the giver two? Wasn't it wonderful that even our lowest-paid employees could afford to give gifts of exceptional quality and style to their loved ones this holiday season?

In a way, Jus, Riggins, and all the hardworking people at Flash were Santa Claus and his elves. I was filled with pride and joy and love at the thought of all the people who were going to be happily surprised on Christmas morning.

Everything was neat and orderly. Calm like the early hours of Christmas morning. Once the doors opened, the crowd would charge in and the jumbling, churning, and bargain grabbing would begin.

There was a method to shopping at the sale. Bring large bags—we didn't provide them. Stuff everything you might be interested in into them. Find an empty space and sort through your finds to make your final selections before you checked out. And remember that money went a long way here. That pile of treasures was certain to cost less than it looked like it should.

This was a strictly cash-only and carry event. No tax. Everything was priced in even dollars. All the money raised went to the children's hospital. It was a win for everyone.

When I was in charge, I was always nervous and eager before a big event like this. Making it successful was my responsibility. But today, I was a basket case of nerves. Talk about holiday stress!

After the sale, Jus and I were hopping on a jet and flying into an impending storm with enough strength to make Santa consider cancelling Christmas. *On Dasher, on Dancer. On Prancer and Vixen. Off to New York to get married!* If only I could have rented a plane named Rudolph for this mission.

The weather report had grown steadily more ominous with each passing day as Christmas grew nearer. The National Weather Service was predicting blizzard conditions in upstate New York by midnight tomorrow, Christmas Eve.

I considered calling the whole thing off. And I'd worked so hard on this Christmas wedding, too. There was nothing I could do. The storm they were predicting was just too strong.

I kept wondering—was the weather too dangerous to chance the trip? Could we beat the storm? Or would it arrive early and strand us in New York?

I'd called the charter company and asked their opinion. They were reassuring. Our pilot was the most experienced in their fleet. Barring some unforeseen change, their detailed weather maps indicated we would be in and out of New York before the first snowflakes before the wild hurricane flew.

Still, I worried. What if we got to New York and were stranded by the storm? What about *The Nutcracker*? And what would we tell our family? How could we explain flying to New York with Dex in the face of the storm of the century?

I took a deep breath. *Breathe. Just breathe.*

I obsessively checked the weather on my phone. I was distracted as I fielded last-minute questions from volunteers.

My friend, Britt, who was helping with the sale, sneaked up on me and touched my arm.

I jumped.

She laughed. "Jumpy, jumpy! Who's supposed to be texting?"

Oops! Almost caught. How would I explain checking the weather in New York?

I slid my phone into my pocket. "Jus said he'd text when he was on his way down." I was becoming a pro at lying.

Britt looked around the room with a pleased expression. "We've done a fabulous job here, if I do say so myself."

I nodded. "Merely fabulous? It's extraordinary! The team really came together." I took a deep breath. "And according to my elves, we managed to grant almost every wish!"

"It took some fast-talking by all of us in merch, and some help from procurement, but yeah, I think we did." Britt grinned.

She'd been my best friend forever. I'd always thought she would be my maid of honor. And done all those maid of honor things. Like keeping me calm and holding my bouquet when Jus and I exchanged rings. Panic. Who was going to hold my bouquet?

But Britt wasn't in on my secret wedding. And Jus and I had promised each other that no one else could know.

One of the volunteers came up to us. "I just peeked out the doors. You should see the line! I've been here every year since Flash started. This is a record crowd. And recordly jovial, too. They've started singing holiday songs."

There was a burst of laughter from outside the doors.

Another volunteer rushed up to me. "It's time. Justin and Riggins arrived a few minutes ago to kick things off."

Britt frowned as she looked at me. "I thought he was supposed to text?"

"So did I!" I laughed to cover being found out. He hadn't promised to text. *Sorry, Jus! I didn't mean to malign your character!*

"That explains the singing! Ten dollars says Jus and Riggins are leading it." I glanced at my watch. "Time to open the doors."

Britt gave my shoulders a squeeze. "What are you waiting for? Let's get this party started." She handed me a silver Christmas bell. "Call your volunteers to order."

I laughed and rang it enthusiastically until the buzz in the room died down. "Everyone ready? It's time to open Santa's Sample Sale for business!"

I strode to the doors and grabbed the handles. "Let the mayhem begin!" I threw the doors open.

Jus and Riggins *were* leading carols. The sight of Jus made my heart squeeze and my pulse race. The guy was hot. And sweet. Totally adorable. The perfect combination. I still couldn't believe that I hadn't seen the possibilities in him in college.

My college self would never believe how life had turned out for us. If I could tell her I was dying to genuinely marry Jus, and worried that a snowstorm would stop me, that I couldn't imagine life without him, that he'd become my best friend, and an excellent lover, she would laugh in my face. And think I was pranking her. It was a lesson I'd learned—never laugh at possibilities and improbabilities. Learn to see past the superficial. And why hadn't I noticed what good basic bone structure Jus had?

Then again, if the college-age me got a look at Jus now, she wouldn't believe her eyes. She would still think I was pranking her.

Jus turned toward the door. Our eyes met. They lit up like always when he looked at me. I didn't deserve that much appreciation and love. I was a lucky girl and I knew it. I didn't take it for granted.

"Santa's main helper emerges!" He gestured toward me.

"Did I miss your holiday speech?" I teased back to him.

Riggins elbowed him. "You didn't miss much! It was pointless. It was boring. But it was short!" He laughed and elbowed Jus.

Jus shook his head. "Are you open for business?"

My volunteers stood at the front of the line, holding the masses back and checking employee badges.

I nodded. "Yes, we are!"

The line erupted in applause and tried to push forward.

"Wait, wait, wait!" I held up my hands, palms out, imitating a traffic cop. They only paused a moment when they heard me holler, "Stop!"

I cleared my throat. "A few announcements before we let people in. The wish fulfillment center is in the back across from the dressing rooms. If you submitted a request for a particular item, look for it there. If it has your name on it, you have first option to purchase it. If you no longer want the item, please let our volunteers know so they can put it out with the general merchandise.

"If you see an item that you requested but it has another person's name on it, I apologize. Some very popular items had multiple requests. We drew names at random to select the winner. In those cases, if the winner doesn't want the item, it will be reassigned to the second person on the list.

"My staff worked overtime trying to make sure everyone got one of the items on their wish list. Happy holidays and happy shopping, everyone!" I stepped out of the way to let the first throng of shoppers in.

Jus came over and gave me a quick kiss. I took his hand and led him into the sale.

He whistled softly. "This looks terrific! Like the mall at the North Pole."

"You've been to the North Pole?"

He laughed.

I shrugged. "I had a little help from the photography and merch departments. You picked up on exactly what I was going for! A festive, mall-quality shopping experience."

He put his arm around me and pulled me close. "You look hot," he whispered in my ear. "Tomorrow you'll really be mine."

I smiled up at him. We never mentioned any hint that our marriage wasn't completely legit when we were in public. We both had a healthy fear of being found out. The constant acting wore on both of us. There was always the fear of slipping up.

"If the snowstorm doesn't stop us." I frowned.

"*Nothing's* going to stop us." His voice was deep and sexy with confidence.

How could he be so sure?

He squeezed me tight. "I have to get back to work."

"Oh?" I said.

He nodded and rolled his eyes. "Another emergency. This one's going to take some time to sort out. I can't bail on Riggins. It's a tech issue. My area of expertise. I'll have to meet you at the plane."

Why was I not surprised?

"Have the driver take you to the airport," he said. "Board the plane. If you get tired, don't wait up. I could be late. Get your beauty rest and take care of my girl." He patted my baby bump.

I smiled at him, loving him beyond reason.

"Dex will meet you at the plane. He can entertain himself." Jus paused. "What's the latest we can take off and still make it to opening bell at town hall?"

"Two a.m. At the absolute latest. Our flight plan calls for one. Which gives a margin of error."

"One. Got it. I'll be there." He winked.

"I hope so. I don't want to have to send Dex after you." I leaned in and whispered in his ear, "No cold feet."

"Have I gotten cold feet yet? I'm the one who conned you into this arrangement." He gave me another squeeze and turned toward the checkout lines by the exit door. "What's that they're giving out?"

"Santa mugs with the Flash logo filled with locally sourced organic chocolates."

"Nice!" He grinned at me and was off, stopping to grab a mug on his way out, and thank and hug the volunteers.

I watched him go, incredibly proud of him. Happy he was mine. As far as any government authority was concerned, Jus was legally my husband. But all I wanted for Christmas was two vows. Mine to him. His to me. Fully sober. Fully in control. Fully present.

As Jus turned the corner out of sight, I pulled my phone from my pocket and checked the New York weather again. The Doppler weather still showed New York in the bull's-eye of a major snowstorm.

And then it hit, the worst storm of the century... There's nothing I can do. We're going to have to cancel our Christmas wedding.

I shuddered. I hoped not. Crap, I hoped *not*.

CHAPTER TWELVE

December 24th, 1 a.m.
Justin
When I boarded the plane, Dex was grating nutmeg onto the foam of a hot cocktail, humming to Christmas music. Kay was nowhere in sight.

"Hey, dude! You made it." Dex slapped me on the back. "Thank God. I was worried I'd have to drag your ass back and defend my cousin's honor. I'm no good at that shit." He sized me up. "You've got too many inches on me to make it a fair fight." He winked. He was bull-shitting.

"Since when do you fight fair?" I said.

He laughed. Neither of us ever fought fair. When you grew up bullied and made fun of for being geeky like we were, you learned to use every trick at your disposal. Mostly you lived by your wits. As far as fighting went, even though he was shorter than me, we were evenly matched.

"Crap, Dex. Why would I no-show? I can't believe Kay"—I searched for the right word—"married me." I'd almost tripped up. Even in the privacy of the plane there was a pilot who could overhear our secret.

As if making my point, the pilot came out and introduced himself. "Ready to take off?"

I shook his hand. "Anytime you are."

He disappeared into the cockpit to get clearance from the tower.

"Dude, you got to stop being so damned grateful Lala stuck with you. She's just an ordinary chick. Tom and Jerry?" Dex lifted a steaming coffee cup up.

"Kay's anything but ordinary." I pointed to the cup Dex held. "A *what?*"

"Tom and Jerry. Whipped egg whites, hot water, booze?" He studied me.

I looked at it blankly.

"Still no recognition? Have you lived under a rock all your life? Geez, I knew you were sheltered, but shit. A guy should know his classic, traditional cocktails." He shook his head and clicked his tongue.

"Oh, yeah." Recognition dawned on me. I must have been tired. "Riggins served those during the Christmas Ship Parade."

"Did he? I knew there was a reason I like that dude." Dex went back to nutmeg grating. "Now that you're part of the family, you have to get with our holiday drinking program." He nodded to the coffee cup. "Our grandpa made these *every* Christmas Eve. It's tradition!" He lifted his arm in the air with flair, accenting his words.

I raised an eyebrow. "Grandpa started making these for his parents' friends when he was eight. Back in the days before electric mixers, when you had to whip the egg whites by hand."

Dex's eyes twinkled as he laughed. "And walk five miles uphill in the snow to school." He sliced a piece of thin fruitcake and held it up to the light.

"What are you doing?" I said.

Dex had peculiar habits.

"And where did you get that?" I didn't stock fruitcake.

"Making sure this fruitcake is thin enough. If you can't see through it, you cut it too thick." Satisfied, he laid the piece on a saucer next to the cup. "I brought it myself. As a special treat."

"I can't believe you eat that crap." I shuddered for effect. "Where are the Christmas cookies?"

"If you think fruitcake is crap, you've never had a good one. This one is made from scratch at a nut farm down south. With their own freshly grown pecans. Try it, you'll like it."

I reluctantly took the cup and saucer from him.

He shook his head at my apparent folly. "I took the liberty of dousing it in a little more rum from the liquor cabinet. Good fruitcake has to be soaked in booze starting just after Thanksgiving. Get it just right, it's better than a rum ball."

I was still skeptical. I took a sip of the cocktail and fell into a leather chair, exhausted.

"Well?" Dex said. "What do you think?"

"Not bad." It was delicious and soothing, strong with brandy. I let the hot alcohol linger on my tongue. "Your grandpa gave you and Kay these?"

"Without the booze. Not bad?" Dex sounded affronted. "Damned by faint praise! I make the best Tom and Jerry on the planet."

"And you're modest, too." I paused. "Watch yourself. There's still time to make the naughty list."

"As if! If I wasn't trapped with you on a jet bound for New York, I'd have a damned good shot at that list." He grinned. "Next year!"

I laughed. "Kay asleep already?"

"She went to bed about an hour ago. No idea if she's asleep. She's nervous about the storm. You being late to the plane didn't help."

"I'm not late." I glanced at my watch. "Just last-minute." I set my drink down. I had no intention of touching the fruitcake. "I'd better let her know I'm here." I rolled my neck. "I'm beat. I'm going to turn in."

He raised an eyebrow and laughed. "Right. I'm sure sleep is the first thing on your mind."

I ignored his innuendo. "You'd better get some sleep, too. We have a big day ahead of us." I grinned. We were alone in the cabin. I whispered to him, "It's my wedding day."

Dex made an exaggerated sigh and shook his head. "You got it bad, boy! This weird arrangement of yours gives you an out. I have no idea why you want to put the last nail in the coffin of your freedom."

I shook my head. "Love is fickle."

Dex grimaced. "Go to bed before you get any sappier. I don't think I can take it." He snatched the piece of fruitcake off my plate. "If you're not going to eat this..."

"Don't stay up too late. And leave something in the liquor cabinet. You're the only witness I have and can trust. I need you completely sober when you do your duty."

"Go to bed, Dad."

Kay was in bed in one of the two bedrooms onboard. The lights were out. The room was dark. Kay was facing away from the entrance.

She turned over when I opened the door. "Jus? You made it." Her voice was soft and sexy with sleepiness.

"Was there ever any doubt?" I slipped out of my clothes and into bed behind her. Just that fast, I was hard and ready for her, pulsing with desire. "I missed you."

"You just saw me this afternoon." Her hair fanned out over the pillow behind her, topped with a sexy red Santa cap.

I ran my fingers through her loose hair. "In the middle of a crowd." I kissed her shoulder. "It's our wedding day."

"Hmmmm," she purred. "Unreal, isn't it?" She turned to face me and put her arms around me.

I tugged on her hat. "What's this?"

"And I in my cap." She pulled my face to hers.

"You're supposed to be in a kerchief."

"Oh? Did I get it wrong?" She pulled the covers back, revealing her beautiful, nearly naked body wrapped in a red satin bow teddy. The top was a push-up bra that showcased her firm, full breasts, tied with a lavish bow. A cross ribbon wrapped over her baby bump and disappeared between her legs.

"What am I supposed to do with this?" I slid my fingers between her legs beneath the ribbon and stroked her until she moaned softly.

"Unwrap me."

"It's not Christmas yet." I kissed the tops of her breasts.

She moved my hand to cover her heart. I felt it beating for me, rapid and excited.

"Doesn't matter. I'm yours now." Her voice was as soft and smooth as the satin of her bow.

Mine, mine, mine. My dick got harder and harder at the thought.

"You're part of my family now," she whispered.

"Not quite."

"Close enough." She kissed me lightly, running her tongue over my lips until I shivered with pleasure. "We open our presents on Christmas Eve. And I do believe it's Christmas Eve now."

"Technically, it's Christmas Eve day. I always open mine Christmas morning. I don't have to unwrap you," I teased, reaching beneath her bra to expose a nipple. "Mere bows are no barrier to me. I can slip past this ribbon no problem."

I slid the ribbon just off center, exposing her outie bellybutton and kissing it. She loved it when I did that. I licked it and sucked on it. I loved her hard, round bump. "No one will know. Except you."

The tip of my dick was wet. She was moist and ready for me. She climaxed almost as easily as I did these days. Hormones, she claimed. I preferred to think it was mad lust for me.

Finding the right angle of entry and position was becoming more challenging every day. A guy had to get creative. And acrobatic.

Past the baby bump, find the slot. Into the spot that made her hot.

I slid Kay to the edge of the bed until she was on her back with her legs dangling over.

I slid to my feet, standing between her legs, looking at this woman who was the best gift in my life. Wondering how a nerd like me had ever won her love. *She loves me.*

The thought always made my heart race and my dick harder.

"What are you waiting for?" she said, egging me on and scooting closer until my dick was pressed against her opening.

"I like to take my time opening my gifts. Wouldn't want to tear the wrapping." I bent down and kissed her, sliding my kisses down her neck to where her pulse beat for me.

I sucked on her exposed breast.

"*Jus.*" She stroked my hair.

As she moaned my name, I speared into her. She was moist and warm, hot and ready for me. That I turned her on like this was another gift I'd never expected.

She gasped and wrapped her legs around my back, her hips rising as I made love to her standing on the floor. As I pounded into her, she moaned.

It was enough to send me over the edge into climax, but I held on. Held out, waiting for her. I set my jaw and drove in again and again. I grabbed her hips to keep her from scooting farther into the bed as I drove into her. And thrust. And thrust as we rumpled the sheets.

Her Santa hat slid off. Her big red bow bounced in rhythm with her fabulous, pregnancy-enlarged breasts.

I was high above her. Looking down. It was a view I could never get enough of. Her face lit up with the pleasure I was giving her. I never took it for granted. I memorized everything about it—the gentle part of her lips. The way she arched her neck and sighed. Her nipples had gotten larger and darker with pregnancy. The exposed one was as round and hard as a holly berry.

Her heels dug into my back, urging me deep and deeper inside. Driving me to keep the pace desperate with desire going.

The muscles of her stomach contracted, making it hard and tight, a beautiful round rock to pound against. Soon the baby inside would rebel and start kicking.

Kay was close. Her eyes rolled upward. She sighed heavily.

I drove harder, grasping her tighter to hold in place on the expensive sheets.

She opened her eyes and stared up at me. "Jus!" She arched and gasped.

I came with an intensity that made me weak in the knees. I shuddered with the force of the climax, standing on legs that became like a bowl full of jelly, quivering. With pleasure and spent lust.

She collapsed, arms overhead, head to the side, breasts heaving. I wanted to hold this picture of her in my mind forever. But damn, it would surely make my dick hard again.

She turned and looked up at me. "That was *wonderful*."

I grinned. "High praise." I'd been a virgin when we married. Insecure because of my inexperience. Kay may have taught me everything I knew about lovemaking. But no one could say I hadn't been an eager student.

I slid out of her and into bed, pulling the sheet and blankets up over our bodies moist with the thrill and exertion of sex. Kay was hot these days. I meant that in the temperature sense, too. She was always flushed. Her cheeks always rosy. Which I found completely sexy.

"So intense," she whispered as she cuddled into me and brushed a lock of hair off my forehead. "So intense since I got pregnant."

"You mean so intense with me?" I teased. But there was a sense of insecurity beneath it. Hard to pound that out of a guy like me that the girls had never noticed until I became rich.

"Yes, *that's* it. That's what I meant. So intense with *you,* Santa baby." She retrieved her hat and slid it on my head, laughed, and kissed me lightly. "You look adorable!"

She paused to study me and laughed again. "It was intense, but then, you're the only guy I've done while pregnant. So I have nothing to compare it to." She winked. She was such a tease.

"You *had* to add that." I leaned on my elbow so I could stare at her and get my fill. "Is that any way to talk to the guy who's going to be your legitimate, legally bound husband in a few hours?"

"Oh, Jus!" Everything about me amused her. "Insecure?" She grinned. "I *love* you. I can hardly wait until you're completely, legally, without doubt, my truly wedded husband."

The tease was still there, but the passion underlying it took my breath away.

She yawned and kissed my shoulder, just a light butterfly brush. "Merry Christmas, you filthy animal."

I smiled. "And a happy New Year." I kissed her again. "I love you, too."

Kayla

Being a pregnant bride was challenging enough. But getting me and my baby bump into a formfitting wedding dress in the confines of a small bedroom on a plane? With only my eager groom to help me? In the middle of the leading edge of an epic snowstorm?

Insane. At least we were on the tarmac. There was no turbulence to deal with as I applied the final touches of my makeup—mascara and lipstick.

The cold wind was not only driving the snowstorm toward us at record speed. It was about to drive me into the edge of madness. And yes, until I'd sent him away to get ready with Dex in the next room, Jus had been helpful. In his sweet way.

He was pretty good with tiny satin buttons. But he was more adept at unbuttoning them than fastening them. And his hands strayed to my breasts at every opportunity. He was merry and bright, a right jolly groom. I was simply a jittery bride.

I'd gotten up in the wee hours of the morning while we were still in the air. I wanted to give myself plenty of time to get ready for the momentous event. And spent an inordinate amount of time trying to make my long blond hair fall into perfect waves over my shoulders and down my back. Jus loved it that way, so I had vowed not to put it up, but wear it to please him.

The wet weather was absolutely going to destroy my cascading locks and render them limp the minute I stepped out of the plane. As long as Jus got a look at me first, though, and Dex snapped a picture, mission accomplished.

My makeup was done by me with care, in hopes that my groom would really stare. Okay, that was bad. But I was nervous and trying to have a sense of humor, however warped, about the whole situation. And failing. I needed one of my grandpa's Tom and Jerrys. A strong one with plenty of Justin's best brandy.

I know. I'm pregnant. Just a sip or two to calm the jitters.

I wouldn't have been nervous at all...it was the storm that was jangling my nerves.

This was the time every girl needed her best friend. I resisted the urge to call Britt. I just wanted to hear her calm voice and wish her merry Christmas Eve. *Uh-huh.*

It was six a.m. in Seattle. She'd be showering for work. Scrubbing with her candy-cane body wash and singing Christmas carols softly off key.

I glanced in the mirror and blotted my lipstick. How I looked didn't matter. How perfect the ceremony was was almost immaterial. Nothing really mattered. As long as we made it to town hall, got our second license, got to the cute little chapel, said our vows, signed the license, and got out of New York ahead of the storm of the century. The odds of us succeeding were looking iffier and iffier with each passing moment and each falling snowflake.

White Christmas, damn that movie, was playing on the TV embedded in the wall. It was like that movie, with its constant plea for snow, had cursed me by doing the celluloid version of a rain dance, conjuring up the frozen stuff instead. What I wouldn't have given for twenty degrees more on the thermometer. Frosty the Snowman could wait until next Christmas season to be kissed by a cold December wind and brought back to life.

The news periodically interrupted Bing, Danny, and Rosemary with dire weather bulletins. Bing Crosby was so happy about his snow. Snow saved the day. Snow. *Snow.* Snow, sung in his low, classic Bingly voice. I begged to differ. I wanted Heat Miser to show up unannounced and give us a tropical heat wave. Just until we were safely wedded and out of town.

I glanced out the plane window at the snow falling, falling, gently falling. Thickly falling. *Incessantly* falling.

My hands trembled as I looked at the weather app on my phone *again*. For the zillionth time. Not to exaggerate or anything.

The storm was moving faster than the National Weather Service had originally predicted. Of course it was! Didn't they have some local news guy on the coast monitoring it like we did back home? Some guy standing in the surf "predicting" the weather, i.e. watching it roll in?

The newscasters were full of jovial excitement. Nothing made their day like a good dire weather story.

Special Alert News Bulletin. We interrupt your regular programing to give you this weather update. Winter Storm of the Century! It will be arriving early, New Yorkers! Lay in your supply of ham hocks and guitar strings. Mush! I said mush.

One hundred percent chance of a white Christmas for upstate New York! Hooray!! Let's hope Santa has Rudolph bridled and ready to lead his sleigh tonight.

Was I the only person on the planet who wasn't dreaming of a white Christmas? This was a complete nightmare. Snow, snow, go away! Come again some other Christmas Day!

All you last-minute shoppers, get your shopping done before noon today. Ha, ha, ha! Run those errands now! The governor is asking businesses to close even earlier than their posted holiday hours. Noon, people, noon. Businesses, show a little Christmas spirit! Let your employees off early. And watch those holiday office parties. The roads will be treacherous.

Later on, build a snowman with the kids. Put a plate of cookies out for Santa. Sit back with a hot toddy, cocoa for the kids or the kid in you.

The governor asks your cooperation in staying off the roads late this afternoon through tomorrow morning. Don't count on the state patrol rescuing you if you get stuck. They'll be busy with only the worst accidents and emergency situations.

You don't want a lump of coal on Christmas morning. Or to be stranded in a ditch on Christmas Eve. And, as a reminder, if you are travelling, carry an emergency kit with spare blankets, water, flares, and food, and make sure your cell phones are fully charged.

The wedding dress I'd chosen was a knee-length white soft jersey sheath tight over my baby bump. It was covered with an intricate floral stretch-lace overlay with elbow-length sleeves and decorated with tiny seed pearls and crystals for shimmer. A wide white satin ribbon tied beneath the bust.

Because we were trying to be stealthy, it looked more like a glistening holiday dress than a wedding gown. I was going to swap the white ribbon for a red one for the ballet. I had a white faux-fur trimmed wool coat and white winter gloves. White boots with a good tread to handle the snow.

I wore the advent charm bracelet Jus had given me. Maybe I'd been wrong about him giving me a Christmas tree bead today. I wondered if he would give me a bridal bead instead? I looked in the mirror and took a deep breath. *Showtime!*

Jus and Dex were waiting for me in the main cabin, sprawled in the deep leather chairs in front of a roaring fake fireplace complete with electronic crackling. So cozy. As long as we've no place to go...

Wait! We had a very important place to go.

When I saw Jus, dressed in his tux, my eyes filled with tears of joy. He was so hot. So handsome. So about to be mine!

When he looked up and saw me, his eyes lit up. "You look beautiful." His voice had that quality of awe that took my breath away. He adored me and wasn't afraid to show it. That kind of emotion was hard to resist it.

Dex got out of his chair and grinned. He shook his head as he gave me a quick up-and-down. "Eh." He shrugged. "She looks all right." He winked.

I sighed, too happy to let Dex's teasing bother me. "You *both* look hot. Even *you*, Dex."

"What do you mean, *even* me?" Dex tapped his chest, pretending to be insulted.

A large red velvet jewelry box wrapped with a satin ribbon sat on the coffee table next to where Jus had been sitting. Next to it lay a large floral box.

Jus picked up the jewelry box and handed it to me. "Merry Christmas, babe."

I looked at him. At it. At him.

"Go ahead. Open it. It's...a present for *both* occasions." He watched me eagerly, still guarding his words.

We were still in secrecy mode. The pilot might hear.

I untied the ribbon, opened the box, and gasped. A sparkling diamond tiara glistened on the satin lining of the box.

"Real diamonds," Jus said, not in a bragging way at all. He was preempting the question I always asked. "As real as my love for you."

I couldn't speak.

"Don't you like it?" His brow furrowed. He was always so eager to please me. "If it's too gaudy—"

"It's beautiful. Perfect and intricate. Delicate." I blinked back tears of happiness. "I love it!"

He took the tiara out of the box. "May I? I'd like you to wear it for the ceremony. I mean, if you want to." He was so adorably hesitant and considerate.

I nodded. "Of course I do! It's just so beautiful. I don't know what to say. Thank you seems inadequate."

Jus sat it on my head, gently working the combs into my hair like a pro. Knowing Jus, he'd practiced this move so he could get it just right. He stood back and admired me wearing it.

Dex had been standing quietly to the side. Totally unlike him. He grunted his approval. "Nice."

I wiped away a tear of joy.

"I bought it before I knew. For the ballet. I couldn't have the Sugar Plum Fairy upstaging my girl."

"No one upstages the Sugar Plum Fairy. But her tiara won't be as nice as mine." I kissed him.

"Guys!" Dex cleared his throat. "I hate to interrupt. But we'd better go before we get snowed in. On the plane and on the tarmac. As much as I'd love a good airport Christmas—"

"We get it." Jus nodded. "One more thing first."

He grabbed the large floral box, opened it, and handed me the most beautiful Christmas wedding bouquet I could have imagined. Red and white roses. Poinsettias. Mistletoe.

I had a bouquet waiting at the chapel. But I wouldn't tell him that. This one was better. Mostly because it came from him.

Jus leaned over and whispered in my ear, "Traditionally, the groom buys the bride's bouquet, right?"

"You've been studying your wedding etiquette," I whispered back. "It's beautiful. Your boutonnieres should be waiting for us at the chapel."

"I wanted our day to be perfect." He grabbed my hand.

"As I long as we say our vows, it *will* be perfect." I took a deep breath.

"Guys?" Dex said again, rolling his eyes. But he was grinning. All this affection no doubt embarrassed him.

I pulled my cell phone out of my purse. "One more thing first—a quick picture. Dex? Take just one?" I handed him the camera before he could deny my request.

He shrugged. "I got this." He leaned toward us and mouthed, "I'm the best man."

Dex snapped a few pictures while we posed, then took a selfie with the three of us. "Never a selfie stick around when you need one."

Dex hated selfie sticks. He handed the phone back to me with the pictures up.

Jus squeezed my hand before I could look at them. "Ready?"

I took his hand, hoping he saw how much I loved him. "As ever."

"Good." He grinned ear to ear. "The car's waiting. Do we have everything? All the paperwork?"

I patted my purse. "It's all right here."

"I called Parson Brown," Jus said with a twinkle in his eye. "He's going to meet us at the venue early. I'm supposed to text him when we leave town hall."

I bit my lip and nodded, grateful to Jus for taking care of that important detail. I'd been worried our celebrant would cancel due to inclement weather. This wasn't a case of we had no place to go. We had the most important place to go.

"And town hall?" I whispered to Jus. "The news is reporting some government offices have decided to shut down for the day. The governor is on the verge of declaring a state of emergency and closing everything."

"Still open." Jus squeezed my hand. "But we need to hurry."

I let out a breath, relieved, and looked heavenward, hoping for a little help warding off the storm. Just long enough for us to get married.

CHAPTER THIRTEEN

Kayla

The pilot came out of the cockpit just as Jus helped me with my coat. "You look like you're going to a wedding! Your own wedding."

I froze.

Jus laughed, nervous as a groom.

Dex shook his head and laughed, too, as he made an exaggerated point of studying Jus, me, and himself. "Ha! Funny! I hadn't noticed. I guess we do."

He gestured to his tux, running his hands in the air past his body with a flourish. "This old thing? This is just our Christmas finery. We always dress up to impress Auntie Agatha when we make our holiday duty call." He lowered his voice. "She's eccentric, but rich. We humor her."

"Mrs. Green is holding a bridal bouquet." The pilot clearly wasn't buying Dex's crazy story.

I was enjoying it, wondering how far he'd take it. I liked the sound of this imaginary Auntie Agatha.

Dex nodded. "Astute of you to notice. A Christmas bouquet for our great auntie. She was married on Christmas Eve to her late husband, Uncle Herman, about what? Seventy years ago now?" He turned to me for confirmation.

I nodded. "About that."

"Before he died, Uncle Herman gave her a bridal bouquet every year for their anniversary. We're keeping the tradition alive, even though Uncle Herman isn't." He glanced at my bouquet. "Auntie loves red roses."

He leaned forward and put a hand to the side of his mouth. "She's ninety-three and a little woo-hoo!" He circled his finger around the side of his head. "We let her believe they're really from Uncle Herman."

Dex handed his phone to the pilot. "Will you snap a picture of the three of us?"

We posed. The pilot took our picture.

Dex thanked him and took his phone back. "Okay, we need to run before we're snowed in. The things we do for family!" He cast a quick glance in my direction, before smiling at the pilot and pointing at the door. "Could you?"

Minutes later, we were out on the snow-covered tarmac in the midst of a raging snowstorm. Plows blew snow high into the air on the next runway over, obviously on a fool's errand. As fast as they plowed, more snow fell and blanketed the ground in white.

Jus paused to give instructions to the pilot. "We'll be back in a few hours at the latest." He glanced at Dex. "Like Dex said, we're making a quick visit to their aunt and then we'll be right back."

The pilot nodded. "I have the tower on standby. They're ready to give us clearance as soon as we're ready to take off. They want everyone they can out of here as early as possible. The sooner you're back, the better. Unless we all want to spend Christmas Eve here on the plane."

Jus nodded and cast a sidelong glance at Dex. "At least if we come to that, we have plenty of fruitcake and brandy." He patted the pilot on the back. "We all want to get home tonight. We have a date with the Sugar Plum Fairy."

"That was close," Jus said when we were out of earshot of the pilot. "I almost blew it with the bouquet. What was I thinking? Nice save, Dex. Agatha?"

"It was the first name that popped into my head." Dex shrugged. "I thought up a lie and I thought it up quick. It's an acquired skill."

"You must be related to the Grinch." Jus grinned.

A four-wheel-drive SUV waited for us at the terminal.

This is it, I thought as Jus handed me into the car. *This is the day I marry the man I love beyond reason, or die trying. Or end up stranded in a ditch with him on Christmas Eve.*

"Take us to town hall," Jus told the driver.

I'd timed everything to the minute. The drive to town hall should have taken us no more than ten minutes. It took nearly thirty. Cars were spun out everywhere. Traffic moved at a crawl. Everyone in the small upstate town was out before they became snowbound for Christmas.

Despite the traffic headaches, our driver was jovial and in the holiday mood.

"This town looks like Bedford Falls," Jus joked as we finally pulled into town. "Where's the old savings and loan?"

"Legend is we were one of the towns the producer based Bedford Falls on." Our driver sounded proud of that fact. "That's town hall straight ahead."

"I don't care about the savings and loan. But we could use an angel like Clarence right now." I squeezed Justin's hand. "Oh, it's lovely!" I exclaimed when we pulled into sight. "Town hall is as quaint as the rest of town."

The driver pulled to the curb. Actually, he pulled to the snowbank that was serving as the curb. Jus paid him generously to wait for us while we went into the quaint town hall building for the license.

Jus helped me out of the car and over the snow bank to a sidewalk that was covered with two inches of snow and had probably been shoveled less than fifteen minutes ago. A wreath was on the door of the building. Inside, it was eerily quiet and nearly deserted. People were closing up offices everywhere we turned."

"We have to hurry!" Jus glanced around. "Where the hell is the office of town clerk? We need a map."

"This place is a maze!" I looked around frantically.

"I'm the best man." Dex spotted a town official heading toward the exit. "I got this." He dashed to the guy and asked him for directions.

The guy pointed. "To the end of the hall. Take a right. Last door on your left. You'd better hurry. We're all closing up shop."

"Thank you! Merry Christmas!" Dex pointed. "This way!"

We took off at a run. Jus pulled me along by my hand holding my bouquet.

"I'm slowing us down!" I said, worried, as I ran with one hand on my baby bump.

"Don't worry! I got you, babe. We'll get there." Jus pulled me faster.

We rounded the corner.

"There it is!" Dex pointed to the end of the hallway. "We're just in time!"

A woman was locking the door to the clerk's office.

"Wait!" Jus called to her. "I'm the groom. I got this." He let go of my hand and took off at a sprint down the hall toward her. "Don't lock up!"

The woman, dressed in an ugly red and green holiday sweater with tacky embroidered reindeer and Santa, the kind that was intentionally ugly, at least I hoped, looked up, startled to see three people dressed for a wedding heading toward her. One sprinting. One running. One waving a bouquet and holding the sides of her belly, which didn't shake like a bowl full of jelly, but slowed me down considerably as I lumbered forward.

The woman frowned. "I'm closing up. We've been ordered home. Because of the storm. You should get home, too."

She was middle-aged and plump. With a kind face.

"Not until we're married. Please." Jus put on his charismatic smile, the one that charmed everyone but the severest Scrooge. "Can you open back up for just a minute and issue us a marriage license? Or find someone who can?

"We have all the paperwork. We'll be fast, I promise. It will just take a second. We'll be eternally grateful. We've flown all the way in from Seattle this morning. We have to get married *today*."

She took the three of us in, including me with my bouquet. Her frown deepened, but she looked sympathetic. When she saw my bump, her expression turned worried. "She isn't going to pop today, *is* she?"

"No." Jus laughed. "Not yet."

"Sweetie," the woman said to me, kindly, but firmly. "I wish I *could* help you. Even if I issue you a license, you *can't* get married today. There's a twenty-four-hour waiting period."

"Oh, but we can!" I dug into my purse, pawing through it wildly, jiggling it enough that my light-up purse jewel flashlight came on. "We have a judicial order setting aside the waiting period. Where is it? Ah! Found it." I pulled the waiver out with a flourish and held it out to her.

She hesitated, looking highly skeptical before taking the order and looking it over. We watched her read, not a creature stirring. When she finished, she still seemed undecided.

Jus put his hand on my bump. "What's your name? We'll name our firstborn after you. We already know it's a girl. Perfect, right? Fate."

The lady's look softened. She shook her head. "My name's Merry. M-e-r-r-y." She sighed and laughed suddenly. "Yes, fate."

She shook her head. "I was born on Christmas Day. The doctor had to fight his way through a snowstorm like this one to deliver me. Looks like it's time to pay it forward. Who am I to stand in the way of true love? Come on in." She pulled her keys out of the door, pushed the door open, and flipped on the light in the dark office.

I almost collapsed with relief. I would have if Jus hadn't been holding me up.

"Perfect!" Jus said. "Her middle name will be Merry."

Merry closed the door behind her and led us to the counter. "I'll need two pieces of ID and the forty-dollar fee."

As we were filling out the paperwork, including the extra piece that specified that the record of our marriage wouldn't be published in a newspaper or any publication other than official records, Justin's phone rang.

He glanced at the caller ID. "Excuse me, I have to take this." He stepped away while Dex signed as our witness.

I heard Jus murmuring in the background.

When he came back, he looked serious and concerned. "That was Parson Brown," he said. "There's a
jackknifed semi blocking the road to the chapel. It
won't be cleared for hours. Maybe not until tonight. Or
Friday."

My face fell. I clutched my belly. I felt sick.

Jus caught my arm. "I'm not done yet. It gets worse.
The parson's road is plowed in. Impassable by car. It
will take him hours to dig out."

"*No.*" If I'd had more strength left, it would have
been more than a whisper of anguish. "But we *have* to
get married! We've come so far!" I was on the edge of
tears.

Jus took my chin and tipped my face up to his. He
was actually smiling. "Don't worry, Kay. Simple change
of plans. Parson Brown will meet us here. He's coming
by one-horse open sleigh. He says nothing will stop his
sleigh. He'll marry us on the town hall steps if he has
to. You picked a good one."

I almost collapsed with relief. "I lucked out. Harry
found him. Parson Brown was the only one in town who
required the second license."

Jus laughed. "Fate strikes again."

We finished with our paperwork without further in-
cident. As Merry let us out of the office, Jus pressed a
handful of bills into her hand.

"No, I can't," she protested.

"Take it. Please. You've made our day. Let me re-
turn the favor." He clasped her hand, pressing it
around the money. "Merry Christmas, Merry! We'll
never forget you."

By the time we reached the doors out of the building, the mayor was waiting to lock up after us. Merry hurried off into the storm to pick her snow-covered car out of the parking lot. The mayor wished us merry Christmas and congratulations and jumped into his idling, warming car to head home.

I stared at the town that looked so quintessentially like Christmas. It belonged on the front of a Christmas card. So innocent and peaceful. So deadly to weddings!

At least four inches of new snow had fallen in the time we'd been inside getting the license. At this rate of snowfall, the plows couldn't keep up. We'd be stranded within an hour.

Our car and driver still waited for us, but the hustle and bustle of the town was dying down as people headed for home and hearth.

And then in the distance, we heard on the road the prancing and pawing of hooves of one great big draft horse, and the jingle of approaching bells.

A sleigh came around the corner. Parson Brown?

He pulled up in front of the steps and jumped out to greet us. He waved with one hand, holding the reins in the other. He cupped one hand around his mouth and called out to us, "Justin and Kayla?"

Jus waved back and nodded. "Come on." Jus pulled me down the steps.

The parson was covered in snow from his head to his toe. A parson's hat sat atop of his head. His cheeks were rosy and red. His dimples how merry. His eyes dark as coal. His beard how it sparkled, laced with snow. He was jolly and round and wore a white puffy down coat with a red scarf around his neck.

Jus grabbed my hand.

As we descended the steps, Dex lowered his voice and spoke out of the side of his mouth. "Is it just me, or does he look like a snowman?"

"Not just you. With that goatee, he looks *exactly* like a snowman," Jus said. "That one on *Elf.*"

"Or like he belongs on a box of fried chicken," Dex added.

"I wonder if he does that on purpose." I marveled at the similarity.

"You aren't pranking us, are you, Lala?" Dex said. "That guy's a real pastor?"

I frowned at Dex. "Seriously? Would I joke about something like this?"

"Sorry. I had to check." Dex grinned impishly. "This is surreal."

It was snowing so heavily that by the time we reached the bottom of the steps, our hair was white with snow. Beneath the streetlights that had come on, my tiara sparkled like the Snow Queen's. And Justin's dark beard was nearly as white as Santa's.

"So this is the happy couple!" Parson Brown formally introduced himself. He sounded astoundingly like an old Kentucky gentleman, rather than a New Yorker. He had that down-home friendliness that put me immediately at ease.

"Okay," Parson Brown said, gazing up at town hall. "So what's the plan? We need to get this show on the road before we get snowed in here."

We nodded.

"First things first," the parson said. "Let's have a look at that license."

Jus handed it to him.

The parson kept talking. "Sorry about the inconvenience of requiring this. This being your second ceremony and more of a recommitment." He held up the license to examine it.

Actually, I was grateful for it. But I couldn't very well tell him why.

"You would not believe the number of couples who come to me to fake a religious ceremony for the relatives, claiming they've already been married in a civil ceremony. And they've done no such thing. Lying to a man of God, right before God!" He shook his snowy head. "Pathetic. Fool me once. Fool me twice? No way.

"Had to start requiring a second license just to make sure I don't get the wool pulled over my eyes again. I'm not going before my Maker having performed illegal weddings." He handed the license back to Jus. "Looks to be in order. Now, where should we perform the ceremony?"

Jus pointed up the steps to the entrance of town hall. "It's covered up there. We have to make it quick. We have a plane waiting at the airport. We need to get out of here as soon as we say 'I do.'"

The parson's gaze followed where Jus pointed. He squinted in thought and nodded. "The airport, you say?"

The three of us nodded in unison.

"I hate to be the bearer of bad news again, kids. But that semi that's blocking the road to the chapel?"

Uh-oh. I had a bad feeling.

"Where it's placed, it's blocking the road back to the airport." Parson Brown hitched a thumb at our waiting SUV. "That car waiting for you?"

"Yes, sir," Jus said, evidently feeling the need to use Southern politeness with this Southern gentleman.

"He isn't going to be of any use to you. Not until they get that wreck cleared. Could be until tonight for that."

Dex swore beneath his breath. "Mom's going to kill me if I don't make it back for Christmas." Then he grinned like it would be a great stunt.

"And we have tickets to the ballet!" I said, as if that was the most important thing.

Parson Brown slapped Dex on the back, catching him by surprise so that he stumbled forward. The parson laughed. "No matter." He pointed to his horse. "Dasher can get you to the airport. He goes overland."

"Dasher?" Dex said. "Seriously?"

The parson laughed again. "What? He's fast!" He nodded to make his point. He looked at Dex. "Can you drive a team? Or rather, a horse-drawn sleigh?"

Dex grinned. "Can I handle a horse and drive a sleigh!"

"I believe that was a serious question." I gave my cousin the evil eye, hoping he wasn't joking this time.

"Yeah! Sure I can." Dex turned to me. "Remember that summer I spent at camp? Horses, no problem."

I wasn't so sure, but Parson Brown seemed to trust Dex.

"Good enough," the parson said. "Here's what I propose. Let your driver go. Then we all hop in the sleigh and I perform the marriage ceremony on our way to the airport while this guy drives." He nodded to Dex. "It's the quickest way to get you on your plane again."

The parson gave me a sympathetic look. "I'm sorry. If you're like most brides, you've probably planned a very nice ceremony. But this will be romantic in its way. It's the best I can do, given the circumstances."

The parson was a very kind, nice man.

Before we even answered, Dex was already climbing into the sleigh.

Jus looked at me for confirmation.

I nodded. "Not many people can say they were married in a one-horse open sleigh in the middle of the snowstorm of the century as they raced to the airport. As far as adventure goes, I defy anyone to top it."

"It loses points for believability, though, don't you think?" Dex said from the sleigh.

"Done!" Jus shook the parson's hand. "Jingle all the way!" He rushed off to pay the driver.

Parson Brown helped me into the sleigh and settled a lap blanket over me before giving Dex a quick driving lesson. By the time he finished, Jus was running back. He hopped over the side of the sleigh with a bound and settled in next to me.

"Very acrobatic," I whispered to him. "You'd make a great elf."

Jus grinned.

"All right, then!" The parson climbed into the front seat next to Dex and gave him quick directions. "Take a right at the first corner."

He pulled a small book of vows out of his pocket. "Okay, now. If it's all right with you two, we'll dispense with the opening remarks and the general charge to you about the solemnity of marriage and the covenant you're about to enter into. I assume you've discovered that by now. We'll skip right to the vows. You didn't write your own, did you?"

Jus and I looked at each other and shook our heads. It was a minor detail I'd overlooked in the stress of the season.

"The basic vows will be fine," I said. "Just as long as the marriage is legal, that's all we care about."

"All righty, then!" The parson clucked to his horse. "On, Dasher! Take us to the airport!" He nodded to Dex.

Dex snapped the reins. The sleigh jolted forward as Dasher plodded off.

"Dearly beloved," the parson began. "We are gathered here today to join this man and this woman in holy matrimony..."

Dasher plodded along down the street. Dex turned the corner.

Parson Brown interrupted the ceremony to give Dex more directions. "Left at the stoplight."

"This would be easier if we used the GPS on my phone," Dex said, pulling it from his pocket as he handled the reins and brushed the snow out of his face. "I'll just punch the airport into my map app."

The parson shook his head. "You won't get directions for the way we're going. No streets for part of it. Most of the roads are closed, like I said. No, we're going to have to go over the river and through the woods."

"Wrong holiday," I whispered to Jus. "That's a Thanksgiving song."

Jus grinned and hummed few bars.

Parson Brown ignored us and kept talking to Dex. "Once we get out of town, it gets tricky. I'll have to take over. Let's get these vows said in a hurry!"

He returned his attention to us. "Where was I? Oh, yes. Justin, repeat after me: I, state your name, take you, Kayla Marie Lucas Green, to be my lawfully wedded wife to have and to hold, to love and to cherish, in sickness and in health, forsaking all others, all the days of our lives."

Jus took my hands in his. As he looked into my eyes and repeated the vows, my heart sang. I blinked back tears. And snowflakes got in my eyes, sticking in my false lashes. But I had never been happier. Jus spoke the words with such passion and intensity. His voice was so deep and full of emotion. I choked up. Then it was my turn.

"I, Kayla Marie Lucas Green, take you, Justin Arnold Green, to be my lawfully wedded husband—"

"Take another left, young man," Parson Brown said to Dex. He nodded to me. "Sorry! Don't want to take a wrong turn and end up in a snowdrift. Continue...to have and to hold..."

I repeated the vows, with all my heart and soul in my eyes and voice. "To have and to hold—"

"Left, left, left!" the parson yelled.

"Sorry!" Dex laughed. "Dasher has a mind of his own."

Course corrected, I continued with my vows, finishing with "...all the days of our lives."

"Rings?" Parson Brown said.

Jus held up his cold, red left hand with his ring. I pulled my glove off and held up my hand, flashing my ring.

"Wearing them," I said. "Should we take them off and exchange them again?"

He nodded. "Hand them to each other. That'll work. Careful not to drop them. Fingers get numb fast in this cold." He watched while we took them off and handed them to each other. "Good, good. Justin, repeat after me. With this ring, I thee wed."

Jus slid the ring on my finger.

"Kayla, your turn." The parson was obviously distracted.

I looked in Justin's eyes and slid the ring easily on his cold finger. Too easily. If we didn't watch it, our rings would fall off.

I looked in his eyes and said the words I'd been dreaming of: "With this ring, I thee wed."

The parson squinted. The snow was falling faster and harder, turning the world whiter, obscuring the path, and decreasing visibility. Parson Brown was issuing more directions and keeping a tight eye on where Dex was taking us. Snowdrifts began popping up out of nowhere, obscuring any landmarks there might have been.

Parson Brown turned back to us with half an ear. "Now, by the power vested in me by the State of New York, and God, I pronounce you man and wife." He turned over his shoulder to make sure we were still on course.

Jus perched on the edge of our seat, waiting for every groom's favorite part of the ceremony.

"You may kiss the bride," Parson Brown said, almost as an afterthought.

Jus took my face gently in his hands. I parted my lips and closed my eyes. Parson Brown took the reins from Dex just as my lips met my real, true, genuine, lawfully wedded husband's.

"Merry Christmas," I whispered to Jus. "I love you."

"This is where we go over the river!" the parson yelled above the joyful jingling of bells. "There's a covered wooden bridge just ahead. On the other side, we cut through the woods. Get out the license and everyone sign!" He pulled a pen from his pocket and handed it to Jus.

"Giddyup!" Parson Brown yelled to the horse. "To the tip of the bridge, to the end of the wall, dash away, dash away, dash away all!"

The sleigh sped up, gliding over the snow. The bells jingled loudly as first Jus signed, protecting the license as much as he could from the wet snow. I signed. Dex signed, protecting the license with his tux jacket. He took the reins again while Parson Brown signed and handed a commemorative marriage certificate around for everyone to once again sign.

"You'll get the real, legal marriage certificate in the mail in six to eight weeks," the parson said as we entered the covered bridge and shook the snow temporarily off.

He folded the real license and gave it a shake in the air. "I'll file this first thing on the Friday, the 26th." He slid it into his inside coat breast pocket. And we were out of the cover and into the snow again.

"Into the woods, into the woods!" the parson said. "This is where it gets tricky. And fun. Hang on!"

And then we were, literally, dashing through the woods.

Jus leaned in and whispered to me, "Did we just get married by a snowman?"

"I think we did!" I was so happy, I started laughing.

Jus joined me.

Dex shook his head. "I get it. Laughing as we go. You guys are crazy." But he grinned.

I turned to Jus. "I love you. Merry Christmas, husband."

Jus brushed the snow off his beard. "I love you, too, wife. You can't imagine how much."

The bells jingled. The snow fell. And I was wrapped in the arms of the man I loved, and was now, finally, *legally* married to.

Jus texted our pilot that we were on our way.

Parson Brown delivered us to the front of the terminal. We wished him merry Christmas and a safe trip back. Jus pressed a generous payment into his hands.

Just as Jus grabbed my hand, ready to race to the plane, a group of high school girls came out of the terminal. I was holding my bouquet.

As Jus pulled me past them, I called out to them, "Catch!" I tossed them my bouquet.

One of them leaped in front of the others and caught it. I got a quick glimpse of her showing it to her friends and laughing before Jus pulled me around a corner.

We raced through the terminal to our gate. Our flight attendant greeted us. Two large coolers and a snow shovel sat at the foot of the stairs up to the plane.

I pointed to them, confused. "What are those for?"

"A white Christmas for Seattle." Jus turned to my cousin. "Dex, get the lids off. Let's start shoveling."

Jus handed me up the stairs.

"Welcome aboard. Watch your step," the new flight attendant warned me as she took my arm. "My name's Jamie. I'll be taking care of you for the flight to Seattle."

"Kayla," I said.

At the top of the step, I brushed the snow off myself and paused to look back at Jus and Dex. They were having a snowball fight. *Guys.*

The pilot greeted me. "The plane's de-iced and ready for takeoff as soon as we load that snow and secure it in the cargo hold."

Jus caught me watching, flashed an apologetic grin, and started shoveling at lightning speed.

Justin

"Buckle up for takeoff." Our flight attendant smiled.

She hadn't been on the flight out. I'd hired her for the flight back. I wanted special service to pamper Kay on the way home. Dinner was going to be late tonight in Seattle. I'd ordered a special inflight meal for us, too. Which should have been delivered while we were getting married.

I sat next to Kay, holding her hand, watching the snow fly past our window as we taxied down the runway. I couldn't stop smiling. This was the happiest Christmas ever.

I relaxed when our wheels left earth and we were finally airborne.

Our flight attendant, Jamie, unbuckled. "You can move about the cabin now."

Dex fired up the fake fireplace. "Time for some refreshments." He rubbed his hands together.

Jamie came over and leaned down to speak to me. "I'm sorry, sir. The meal and cake you ordered weren't able to be delivered because of the storm."

I nodded. "Thank you. Don't worry about it."

"We *were* able to get some nice commercial meals from the airport food services," Jamie said. "But no cake. Really sorry."

I looked at Kay and held my hands palm up.

She laughed. The snow had melted in her hair and taken the curl out. The tiara sparkled in the fake firelight. But at least that was the only thing that was fake now. Her cheeks were rosy and her hands red as she warmed them. She had never looked more beautiful.

"No cake? What do you mean no cake?" Dex jumped to his feet.

Jamie looked alarmed. "I'm sorry—"

Dex went to the kitchenette and pulled his fruitcake from the fridge. "What do you call this!" His eyes shone with triumph.

"Inedible," I said.

"Oh, no!" Kay laughed. "Irreconcilable differences already! I *like* fruitcake."

I rolled my eyes. "That's because you're pregnant. Have your weird food cravings started again? Would you like a pickle with that?"

Dex shook his head at us and pulled out a knife. "I'll just cut us each a nice, thin slice." He paused with the knife poised over the cake. "You know in Britain, fruitcakes are wedding cakes." He spoke casually, like he was just being his usual know-it-all self. But he raised one eyebrow significantly.

"Thank God we're not British!" I shuddered for effect. "What's next? Figgy pudding?"

"A fruitcake makes a *lovely* wedding cake." Kay's eyes sparkled with affection for her cousin. "Most of them are frosted, though, aren't they?"

"That's just...disgusting," I said.

Dex ignored me and held the knife out to Kay. "Why don't you two do the honors?"

Kay took my hand, pulled me to my feet, and dragged me over to the cake. "Enough bah, humbug! Come on, Jus. It's Christmas Eve. For me?"

I grinned. "I can't refuse you anything."

We held the knife together and sliced a very thin slice of the cake, flipping it onto a plate.

Kay broke a piece off and held it up to feed to me. "Try it, you'll like it." She whispered, "It's tradition, Jus."

What could I do? I opened my mouth and braced for the worst. When it hit my tongue, I was pleasantly surprised. "Not bad. Dex dousing it with my best brandy helps!"

"You love it and you know it!" Kay said as I broke off a piece to feed to her.

"Oh, this is delicious." She closed her eyes, savoring it. "This is a good one, Dex! Nut farm?"

Dex beamed as he nodded. "Ha!" He pointed at Kay and then at me. "My cuz knows her fruitcake and has impeccable taste. In everything but men." He laughed. "Recently that's improved, too."

He pulled the bottle of champagne from the ice bucket I'd requested Jamie to chill for us, and popped the cork. He poured three glasses and handed us each one.

"Merry Christmas!" He raised his glass in a toast. "To happily ever afters."

We clinked glasses. Kay sliced us each another piece of fruitcake.

As we settled down in front of the simulated roaring fire for the rest of the flight, I turned to Kay. "Let it snow. Let it snow all it wants now."

She smiled at me. "Now that we've no place to go but home! Sing it for us, Jus!"

CHAPTER FOURTEEN

Kayla
We had to stop in Ohio to refuel and de-ice the plane. We were delayed there several hours by the edge of the big storm, putting us into Seattle just half an hour before showtime.

The ballet closed and locked the doors once the performance began. If we missed the opening, we wouldn't be allowed in until intermission.

I dried my hair on the plane and restyled it. I touched up my makeup and swapped out my white ribbon for red and my boots for heels.

As I got ready, Jus freshened up, too. He kept nuzzling me while I tried to get ready. And I kept staring at that tiara and touching it. I couldn't believe it was real. I couldn't believe we were really married.

"We did it!" I said when we were alone in the bedroom of the plane. I was giddy with joy and relief. "We really did it! I didn't think we were going to for a while. Everything was against us. But you"—I kissed him—"you were magnificent! I was a wreck."

"You were beautiful." He kissed my neck.

"Jus?" I said. "What are you going to do with that snow?"

"Dump it in your parents' yard, right by the front door just before we arrive there tonight. I paid some guys to do it for me." He kissed me again. "It's our cover story for the night. We were making a white Christmas for them."

"And we couldn't rent a snow machine?" I said. "We had to fly into a snowstorm why?"

"Because it's a whole lot more fun. Snow machines don't work fast enough to get it to really pile up. Not when the temperature is above freezing." He caught me in his arms. "And I had important business to take care of in New York."

"Did you?" I laughed again as he kissed me.

Traffic was heavy on the way to the ballet. The car dropped us off at the front door. Once again, Jus grabbed my hand and we ran for it. We made it to the inside theater doors just as they were closing.

"Wait!" Jus called out. "We're coming! Don't close yet!"

"We're beginning to make a habit out of this," I said to Jus.

He grinned as we slid in the door just in time.

"Thank goodness!" my mom said as we walked into the box and the lights dimmed. "I didn't think you were going to make it."

I didn't, either.

My mom smiled at me. "You look beautiful, Kayla! Almost like a bride."

My heart stopped for a minute. I squeezed Justin's hand. We exchanged a quick, knowing glance. I smiled back at my mother. "Thanks, Mom."

Justin's mom frowned at him. "Where were you? I was getting worried."

Jus squeezed my hand and smiled at me. "Taking care of business, Mom. Just taking care of business."

She looked at us like we were crazy. And in truth, we were both smiling like we were fools.

Jus leaned down and hugged his mom. "Merry Christmas! Merry Christmas, one and all!" He laughed as he smiled at me again and gave me a quick kiss. "Merry Christmas, *wife.*"

Gina Robinson is the award-winning author of the contemporary new adult romances *Rushed, Crushed, Hushed, Reckless Longing, Reckless Secrets,* and *Reckless Together* and the Agent Ex series of humorous romantic suspense novels. She's currently working on the next Jet City Billionaire romance.

Connect with Gina Online:
My Website: http://www.ginarobinson.com/
Twitter: @ginamrobinson
Facebook: www.facebook.com/GinaRobinsonAuthor

www.ingramcontent.com/pod-product-compliance
Lightning Source LLC
Chambersburg PA
CBHW070839120626
46556CB00002B/803